THE IVORY WAR

ALSO BY PAUL BENNETT

NICK SHANNON THRILLERS
Book 1: DUE DILIGENCE
Book 2: COLLATERAL DAMAGE
Book 3: FALSE PROFITS
Book 4: THE MONEY RACE
Book 5: BLUE ON BLUE
Book 6: SHANNON'S LAW
Book 7: SHANNON'S GAMBLE
Book 8: SHANNON'S REBIRTH
Book 9: SHANNON'S TRIAL

JOHNNY SILVER THRILLERS
Book 1: MERCENARY
Book 2: KILLER IN BLACK
Book 3: ONE BULLET TOO MANY
Book 4: NO EASY WAY OUT
Book 5: THE IVORY WAR

STANDALONE NOVELS
CATALYST

THE
IVORY
WAR

PAUL BENNETT

Johnny Silver Thriller Book 5

Joffe Books, London
www.joffebooks.com

First published in Great Britain in 2024

Cover art by Nick Castle

ISBN: 978-1-83526-585-7

PROLOGUE

Sierra Leone

A lifetime ago

Some people will do anything for gold. Kidnap, maim, torture and kill. A rich menu to choose from. And wherever there is gold, it will need protection. That was why we were here.

We were a tight-knit group of five mercenaries led by myself, Johnny Silver, black sheep of the Silvers' investment bank dynasty. I had taken the rap for a younger brother, Carlo, on a deal that went wrong and cost the bank a lot of money. Carlo never spoke up and I was sent into exile. Having no real family left to me, I went back to my half-blood roots and joined the Israeli army. Trained to kill by my newly-adopted military family, I left to become a mercenary and worked in Europe for a while, until disillusionment kicked in.

On my travels, I met the best friends a man could want. The one who handed me a beer was called Bull, a six-foot-six Jamaican. He sat down beside me under the shade and leaned back on a smooth rock. I took a sip at the beer and wished we had a fridge. I looked over the landscape of the eastern region of Sierra Leone, poor farming land but rich in minerals. Nestled in the mountains was the gold mine we were protecting. It was owned by the local tribe, which meant nothing to a band of brigands that regularly swooped down from the hills to raid the coffers.

'Amazing,' said Bull. 'All this wealth and they still live in huts. Maybe if we get rid of the bandits, they could build something of bricks and concrete. Something permanent. Build a school for the kids, maybe. A health clinic, too.'

I shifted the bulk of the Kalashnikov on my knees into a more comfortable position. My favourite weapon was an Uzi (Israeli-made, lighter, less prone to jam) but there were none here. Kalashnikovs were ten a penny, thanks to past Russian interventions, and were what Stanislav had sourced. He had also somehow got hold of one Dragunov sniper rifle and five Browning Hi-Power handguns with shoulder holsters. Great work again from Stan the Plan. I looked after strategy, while he worked on tactics. He was Polish, tall and with a deep, melancholy voice — and reminded us annoyingly at every opportune moment that Poland had the best vodka and pickled gherkins in the world. Not much of a diet, but I took his point on the vodka element at least.

I shaded my eyes and looked at the sun shining over the hills and casting shadows on the mine workings. It was a pretty picture, if you liked barren. There was the black hole where men were entering the mine with planks of wood to shore up the latest seam they were working on. The temperature was high and the air was so heavy with humidity that you could take a handful, squeeze it and water would come out — metaphorically speaking, but you get the picture. The monsoons would be coming soon, and that would signal the end of our contract. We had been paid half upfront in dollars. No one dealt in the local volatile currency of leones, and certainly not us.

Pieter came out of one of our tents and handed me a plate, which was supposed to be lunch.

'Any meat in the rice today?' I asked, knowing the answer.

'Not that I found. Maybe there'll be steaks in the evening.'

'One can only hope.'

Pieter was South African, and had done his time in the army there before he went freelance as a mercenary. He was tall with blond hair, long eyelashes and vivid green eyes. He dealt with any females we came across. In our travels, we had been involved in many fights over the besmirched honour of daughters and wives. In company, we watched him like a hawk. But he was effective and persuasive among the women we came across.

The last member of our crew was called Red. He was a Texan with half-Comanche blood. He had black hair and a dark face. Given the opportunity, he would regale us with folk myths of past Native American legendary heroes, which none of us believed.

'We have to get out of here,' he said. 'No proper food, no chilled beer, no action.'

'Action might be coming,' I said. 'The monsoons will make life difficult for the natives here, and the bandits, too. It will turn everything into a quagmire. If there is no attack before the rains, then it won't come before the new season.'

'I'm getting stir crazy here. I'll take the jeep and do a circuit of the grounds. Anyone want to join me?'

There was silence. Red was the fastest driver I'd ever met, but not the most careful. The best strategy was to hang on to something and silently pray to whatever god was yours — or maybe all of them, to be on the safe side.

'I'll come,' said Bull, to avoid the embarrassment of no volunteers. Then he spoilt it. 'I'll drive.'

'I'll do a round of the firing positions,' said Stan.

Every morning and evening, Stan would tour firing positions that he had prepared as his first task on arrival at the camp. There were two sets that had been laid out, one at our first distance and another much closer. Each position provided cover through a mound of rocks and allowed the maximum arc of fire. Every one had a bottle of water and two clips of bullets for the Kalashnikovs. He didn't need to do it so regularly, since there had been no change in our circumstances, but he was a perfectionist, and we had been glad of that many times in the past.

'What are we going to do when this contract ends? Something a lot less basic would be much appreciated,' Pieter said.

'Find some more innocent people to protect,' I replied. 'There's a lot more mining goes on in Sierra Leone. The country is rich in diamonds. Maybe just move on to one of those mines.'

'Our options are limited,' he said, 'since we always need to fight for the good guys. Not that I'm complaining.'

We had done a tour of Europe and fought there many times. Unfortunately, it was impossible to work out who were the good guys and who were the bad. As a mercenary, you had to have a code that you could live by. Otherwise, you would be just animals.

'Maybe we could take a holiday. A little respite. Recharge the batteries. It's easy to get jaded without a break every now and again.'

'Do we have the funds for that?' Pieter asked.

'We've got the first payment on this contract. Money in the bank and the second half to come. Enough so we can relax for a while. Assess the situation. I hear Angola, too, is rich in diamonds. We might be able to pick and choose the next job.'

'I'd give a lot for some steak,' Pieter said. 'Not to mention some female company. It's like they have put a lock and key around the women here.'

'Your reputation must have preceded you,' I said.

Suddenly, Stan came running back. 'Dust on the ridge,' he called. 'Firing positions!'

I slung the Kalashnikov over my shoulder, picked up the sniper rifle and ran to the foremost of the first set of positions — a good general leads from the front. Pieter took a position a little back on my right, and Stan on my left. I could now see

4

our jeep speeding back. Bull and Red would slot in behind us at the two rearmost points. Finally, we had action. Time to earn our keep.

Three large trucks screeched to a halt in front of the entrance to the mine, presumably hoping the shock would render the village men petrified and compliant. We had given orders that when the bandits came, the workers should move to the back of the mine, safely away from the fray.

About fifteen men disembarked from the trucks and stood in a group. I waited to see who took command. A man was waving his arms and the bandits moved into three smaller groups, so that they surrounded the mine entrance on the three open sides. I had my target.

I picked up the sniper rifle. The Kalashnikovs had a theoretical range of 800 feet, but the accuracy at that distance was poor. The Dragunov also had that range but, with the telescopic sight and spiral barrel, was a precision tool rather than a blunderbuss with bullets going all over the place. I lay down, lined up the rifle and aimed at who I supposed was the leader.

The man was still waving his arms to order his men. I held my breath to steady the rifle and let off three bullets — one would have been enough, but I wanted to create some noise and confusion among their ranks. The leader dropped to the floor.

I switched to the Kalashnikov and ran to the foremost position on the nearer set that Stan had laid out. The others moved behind me. We now had the distance from the bandits for the Kalashnikovs to be accurate enough. We all opened fire.

My instruction to the crew was to shoot at the legs of the bandits to reduce the death toll to manageable proportions — only shoot to kill as a last resort. We were not butchers. Honour must be preserved.

The burst of shells caused mayhem. Three men in the middle went down and the rest scattered in all directions. We picked them off one by one, each shell knocking them down by its sheer force. You could literally cut a man in half with one burst. Note that I didn't use 'metaphorically' this time. The Kalashnikov is a cruel weapon.

One man opened the driver's door of one of the trucks. I shot his legs before he could get in. With no escape, hands went in the air. They had had enough.

We stood and walked the short distance to the mine.

'Drop your weapons! Hands on heads.' I didn't know how much English they knew, but there was a compliance.

I went to the mine entrance and called inside for the village chief.

A man, shaken, came out.

'It's safe,' I said. 'I want you to interpret.'

He nodded.

'This is what to say: "You are thieves and robbers. You have been taught a lesson today. Remember it well. If you try to come back, then we will kill you instead of aiming at your legs. Come back and die, or ride on. It is your choice. Don't make the mistake of forcing us to kill you. It is certain death. Now, get everyone into the backs of the trucks and go."'

I counted ten of the men who needed help to get in the vehicles. It would be a long trip to a hospital to take out the bullets — those that hadn't gone straight through. There was a struggle from the remaining five standing to drag the fallen to the trucks and lift them inside. We kept our weapons trained on them in case anyone decided to be a hero. Didn't seem likely, but you never knew. Be prepared, as the Scouts say.

The workers came out of the mine and danced in celebration, shouting curses at the bandits. One of them kicked at a bandit lying on the floor. I shouted at him and he stood back. Honour said that he should stand back rather than take more revenge for the raids over the years.

The village chief shook my hand with a pumping arm and smiled. I reminded him of our deal and asked for the remaining balance now that the job was over — the bandits wouldn't be coming back.

He frowned for a moment then smiled again. He said he had no more dollars, but would pay us in gold, which could easily be turned into cash at Freetown. We'd just have to trust him.

He went inside the mine and returned carrying three large rocks with gold seams shining brightly within them. Stan took care of them, and we went to our room and packed our bags. One of the villagers would drive us to Freetown so that he could bring the truck back.

It was a three hour drive and we laughed at how sweetly the win over the bandits had gone. The adrenaline flowed and we were in post-battle euphoria. Stan said he was ready for a large injection of vodka, and Pieter said a steak was what he was longing for. Bull voted for both and no pickled gherkins. I was yearning for a hot shower. Red just banged his hands at the side of the truck, frustrated by the slowness of the driver. We had to restrain him from stopping the truck and jumping into the driver's seat.

Freetown was bustling, the streets heavy with traffic running slowly between the developed areas and those of centuries past. We told the driver to drop us off at the best hotel. We disembarked and stretched our legs. I took the nuggets from Stan and went to find the nearest gold merchant.

A small man with round spectacles with heavy lenses smiled at me and inspected our rocks.

He laughed.

I asked him how much they were worth.

'Nothing.'

'Nothing?'

He explained that they were what was called fool's gold. Just plain iron pyrites.

And the moral of this story?

Sometimes there are just no good guys.

CHAPTER ONE

The island of St Jude, Caribbean

Now

Bull and I sat under a shade outside my beach bar on the paradise island that was St Jude. The sun was shining as it always did, the sand was golden as it always was, the palm trees at forty-five degrees as they always were. What was there not to like?

The sign on a piece of driftwood said *Johnny Silver, proprietor*, and I was proud of it. It didn't look much, but it was mine, home to my wife, Anna, and our two children. Bull and I had completed our morning ritual of thirty minutes swimming and then a run back along the beach. Bull led me on swimming, where the result of being hamstrung by the Russians didn't impede him too much. I caught him up on the run back, where the old injury in my left shoulder, caused by six bullets tearing away at the muscles, didn't come into the equation. That was from years ago, in our mercenary days. Now, we were changed individuals. Retired and extremely happy. Life couldn't get much better.

The bar had a decent custom. There was only one hotel on the island and it was five-star and expensive. Visitors came for the luxury and soon got bored — there's only so much scuba diving and flunkies with napkins folded over their left arms one can experience. That's where Bull and I came into our own. I provided the simple pleasure of beers, cocktails and flying-fish sandwiches outside their clinical restaurants and bars. Bull did a trade in taking visitors on game-fishing trips from his boat. Neither of us needed to work — we'd made a packet from our taking down of the Russians — but it was pleasure to the highest degree, and there was no need for any distractions from proper nine-to-five work. As non-executive director of the family business of Silvers, the investment bank, I went to London for two days a month around board meetings. Apart from that, I revelled in the easy life and my happy family.

I rolled the beer bottle on my forehead and smiled.

'Same old busy day,' Bull said.

It was Monday, and the guests would have had two days of luxury and would be starting to get bored. It was itchy-feet time. Ethnic was what they craved now. Good for them. Here we come.

I went behind the bar and, before opening up, changed from my swimming costume into a pair of shorts and a light-blue T-shirt with our name and logo on it. Spare expense? Not us.

'Trade coming,' Bull said as a clutch of people appeared from the direction of the hotel.

I ran my fingers over the Browning Hi-Power 9mm handgun taped under the counter. Old habits die hard. I'd had to resort to it once in the past. As for the future, you never knew. *Play safe, Johnny.*

A group of eight people walked along the sand. I predicted daiquiris for the women and marlin for the men.

'What will they catch today?' I pulled back the front of the bar to reveal the treasures within.

'Depends how much they pay,' Bull said. 'Are they gonna be mean with the price or not? I can't get into this haggling business. I cut them ten per cent if they seem to look like nice people and big tippers. Marlin for those who behave themselves and aren't stingy. Zilch for the rest.'

Bull knew the fishing grounds like the back of his hand and would pick the spot according to the attitudes of those paying. Whatever, they would have a good time. I would supply the drinks and sandwiches and Bull the inspiration.

The men were dressed in shorts — no T-shirts, which could well be a problem for hours out of the shade on the boat. A price was agreed, and Bull sent them back for shirts and lots of factor fifty. Departure, thirty minutes.

The group moved over to me, the girls, in their bikinis and sarongs, finally dragged away from admiration of Bull's physique. I could tell that the men were not too pleased, so I served them beer to placate them, and daiquiris for the women. Good start to the day, if a little early — but who was I to judge? The sun must be over the yardarm somewhere in the world. All seemed to be going well. Seemed. They took seats in the morning sun, and I waited for action, which wasn't long.

'Are you looking at my bird?' said one of the men, the unanswerable question like Morton's fork, a no-win situation. If you said no, the response would be something like, 'Is she not good enough for you?' If you said yes, it was like, 'Making eyes at her, are you? Trying to steal her away.'

Which was the last thing on my mind, married as I was to a real contender in any beauty pageant, and this girl was Plain Jane. Apart from the breast enlargement, that is. Big as a defensive weapon. I wondered how she could manage to stand upright.

It was a paradox. No answer would result in anything less than an argument.

Bull caught my eye. I shook my head to say I could handle this.

'Good question,' I said to the belligerent man. 'You win a beer. Or can I interest you in something more local? A shot of rum over ice?'

10

I took off my T-shirt and turned my back to him.

He gasped.

'Do you think you can do more damage to me than that?' I said.

There was a pause.

'I'll take the rum option,' he said.

'On the house.'

We shook hands. Best friends now that the alpha-male thing was over. I poured him a rum on ice and placed it on the bar.

'This is for sipping,' I said. 'Finest in the Caribbean. Roll it round on the tongue. Nectar.'

'How did you get the scars?' he said. 'If you don't mind me asking.'

'Argument with a Kalashnikov, and the Russian who was handling it. It's a long story. Maybe ask Bull, if there's a lull in the fishing.'

I started to make up the package for their fishing trip, heating up the grill for the flying-fish sandwiches while I put the beers and lots of water in one cool bag. The sandwiches would go in another. I slipped ice packs in both. Bull came over, ready to pick up the bags and carry them back to the boat.

Only the men were going fishing: the women would stay drinking at my bar and talk until they got giggly and wove their way back to the hotel for a couple of paracetamols and a nap.

Bull and the party boarded the boat and prepared to leave. I gave him the thumbs up that they would be no trouble, information from me that he could use to set the end price for the trip and choose a good fishing ground.

Anna joined me at the bar. The children, twin girls, were at nursery, so she had some free time. She would serve drinks while I restocked the fridge after the previous evening's delivery. Originally from Chechnya, she had long dark hair bleached blonde by the sun, which was scraped back in a ponytail, revealing her fine bone structure and the full beauty of her blue eyes against her tanned face. She was wearing a pair of white denim shorts over her long legs and a crop top that showed her flat tummy and would be cool as the heat built in the day. Her beauty always drew gasps from the men and jealous frowns from the women.

I was halfway through my task when my cell phone rang. I looked at the screen and saw it was Pieter calling. Unusual.

I walked to the back of the bar and answered it. 'Pieter. Great to hear from you.'

'You may not think that when I tell you the reason for the call. I've got trouble and I need some help.'

I walked outside and sat down under a shade. 'Fire away.'

'I'm a ranger for a private safari reserve in South Africa now,' he said. 'There's too much poaching going on. Elephant and rhino tusks mainly, but anything that contains ivory, even hippo teeth. It's getting out of control. The local guides can't stop it — I think they may be taking bribes. It's too much for me to handle on my own. I need help, Johnny. The effect on the local wildlife is devastating. Today there was another dead elephant. A mother, too. The baby won't survive without her. It's out of control.'

The five of us were a kind of mercenary version of NATO. When one of us was attacked, all of us would join forces against the bad guys. You never had to face danger alone. It was an unbreakable pact.

'I'll rally the troops,' I said. 'Stan will need some details about resources. Will you supply weapons, or will he need to source them?'

'I can get all we need,' Pieter said. 'Even an Uzi for you — I know that's your favourite. Handguns, Kalashnikovs, sniper rifles, the lot. I've got good connections with a gun shop. Tell Stan he doesn't need to worry about that.'

'What else should we be bringing, bearing in mind we'll all be flying and searched at the airport?'

'Just yourselves. Cool clothes would be good. High season here. Camouflage would be best. I'll fix accommodation, although that might be basic.'

'I imagine we will need at least three days before we can get to you. Try and hold out till then. We're coming.'

'I'll text you the details as to where I am, and I'll stand by waiting. And, Johnny, thanks. I didn't know what you would say. I'm humbled.'

'There was never any doubt,' I said. 'Hang in there.'

Pieter cut the call and I started to think about logistics. We'd missed the hotel's courtesy morning boat to Barbados, the nearest place where we could get a flight to South Africa, either direct or through some hub like Heathrow or Schiphol. I would have to get approval from Anna and fix up cover for the bar — there was an old sea-dog called Tobias, a grizzled man with skin like leather, who looked like Popeye the Sailor Man, even down to the pipe. He was reliable, and customers liked him for the local colour. Couldn't ask for better in any emergency. I could then move on to summoning Red and Stan and booking flights for Bull and me. Afternoon? Packing, although that wouldn't take long, seeing that I always kept a giant Bergen rucksack packed with essentials for emergencies. The rest of the day? Worrying, I expected.

Anna looked at me with a frown. 'It's trouble, isn't it?'

'Pieter's got a problem,' I said. 'I'll need to be away for a few days.'

'Any chance of me persuading you to change your mind? That your mercenary days were over? That you would be years older and wiser? That you might not be able to cut it like the old days?'

'We always knew that there would be a day like this. Responding to a call for help. I have to do this. I couldn't live with myself if I turned him down.'

'It's that thing about honour, isn't it?' she said.

I nodded. 'To not help him in his hour of need would be dishonourable. He came to my aid when I needed it. I have to do the same for him.'

'Then go with my blessing,' Anna said.

CHAPTER TWO

Bull and I sat in first class on the plane to Heathrow, where we would transfer to a Virgin Atlantic flight to Johannesburg, and then to a local flight to get us to the safari lands of Eastern Cape. It would be a long, hard haul, and I hoped we'd have time for some recovery from being sedentary for so long and get acclimatised to the new time zone before the action started.

It had to be first class — no way could Bull fit into an economy seat. We drew furtive glances from other passengers. It wasn't due to the casual clothes we were wearing. It was our eyes. There was a glint of steel in them. It would be the same for Stan and Red. There was death in them. It evoked danger. It said *Don't mess with us or you'll regret it.* No one wanted to linger over that look. People quickly turned away.

You are supposed not to drink alcohol when flying, so Bull and I were sipping a glass of the complimentary champagne. Champagne doesn't count. Just fizz, that's all.

'Are you nervous?' Bull said.

'About flying? No, I do it frequently now.'

'You know what I mean,' he said. 'About action. Stepping back into our mercenary shoes. The last time we met up, Red's eyesight wasn't as good.'

'Then we give him a shotgun and put him on the back door of our formation.'

'Pieter had put on weight.'

'Then we get him doing exercise every day.'

'Maybe I've lived too long in a relaxed life, and my reactions have got slower.'

'You'll do,' I said.

'Can you still cut it?'

'I'll worry about that when the time comes.'

'You seem to have all the answers.'

'Only if you ask the right questions.'

He shook his head. 'Sometimes you crack me up, Johnny,' he said, 'but not this time. Maybe if I have some more champagne, I might get inside that mind of yours.'

'I wouldn't bother,' I said. 'Not worth the effort. I gave up trying to do that years ago.'

Bull picked up his empty miniature bottle of champagne and showed it to the female member of cabin crew. She ducked back into the crew area and appeared instantly to bring us refills.

'Are we there yet?' Bull said.

'That's an old one,' I said. 'We've been there before.'

'Remind me?'

'You say, "Are we there yet?" and I say, "No." Two minutes later, you ask the same question, and I say no again. Then you repeat it every five minutes until I'm debating whether to slit my wrists.'

'I didn't realise I was so predictable.'

'Don't change,' I said. 'It's one of the things I like about you.'

'OK, What about this? I spy, with my little eye, something beginning with "P"?'

'Plane,' I said.

'Correct,' he said. 'You're good at this. Your turn.'

'I'd like to quit while I'm ahead. How about seeing who could last the longer without speaking?'

'Doesn't sound very exciting.'

'Hard to beat "I spy".' I closed my eyes and pretended to sleep. It wasn't very convincing because of the regular need to sip more champagne before it went warm. We were quiet for a while. Thank goodness. Bring on the action. Bring on everything.

* * *

Heathrow was the usual drag, with queues throughout and no reassurance that we and our luggage would arrive safely and together at the other end. Luckily, we did. The journey to Joburg was fine, and we didn't drink the Virgin plane dry.

The final link from Joburg to the local airport on the East Cape was frightening. It was one of those old Fokker Friendship dual propeller planes which should have been retired decades ago, and had room for only twenty-one passengers. There was a configuration of two seats on the right on each row and seven single seats on the left. We flew low and caught the turbulence at that level. The only consolation was that Bull could stretch his legs on one of the front seats. No one seemed to mind switching seats for some strange reason.

Pieter met us when we landed, and he looked well. Tanned face, blond hair with just a touch of grey, blue eyes still sparkling. He was wearing beige chinos and a short-sleeved shirt of the same colour. Fittingly, he was dressed for a safari.

'You've added a bit of weight, my friend,' I said.

'Too much sitting around in a jeep and not enough walking,' he said. 'Before you say it, I know that will mean some early morning sessions with Bull, and I'm all right with that. Good to see you both again. Stan and Red arrived this morning and I have saved a full briefing for this evening over a cold beer. Won't be long now. The sun goes down quickly here.'

Bull sat in the front passenger seat and I sat in the back, which wasn't actually big enough to call a seat as the boot was enormous and took up space that could have been used by a passenger. The sky was bright and there were no clouds.

Looked like a good climate. I could see why, with the added extra of the safari, it would be a favourite for tourists.

We were in a flat grassy plain, which gave way to shrubland and then trees and led up to a range of hills where bigger carnivores could lie in wait, camouflaged against the backdrop.

'To the north of us,' Pieter said, 'lies Kruger National Park and above that is the Kalahari Desert. There's another game reserve to the north as well. The climate is mainly temperate, although the weather is changing due to global warming — hotter, with more rain. The grazing animals like it, as it makes the savannah more lush.'

'Tell us about the animals,' I said. 'Presumably, that's why people come here. A big adventure rather than being stretched out on a lounger in the sun with a cold beer, enticing as that is.'

'It's the Big Five,' he said. 'Lion, leopard, rhino, elephant and buffalo. You can see them all here. Plus, there's other animals. Like hippos, which for some reason aren't included in that classification. Holiday of a lifetime. Makes the country rich. Mining, too — gold, platinum, chrome and other valuable minerals — but that's not scenic. Visitors hardly ever go there.'

'How's it off for champagne?' Bull asked. 'I've got a taste for that, after our treatment on the planes.'

'Then you're in luck,' said Pieter. 'Champagne, red and white wines are plentiful here. Take your pick or, better still, try them all. You're going to love this place.'

Except it's going to involve some fighting, I thought. It would be another Mrs Lincoln moment — 'Apart from that, Mrs Lincoln, how did you like the play?'

'What about diseases? What might we pick up while we're here?' I said. 'Bearing in mind none of us have had time for any jabs or other medications.'

'Nothing to worry about,' said Pieter. 'This is not a malaria zone. Nothing else to worry about either. You'll be looked after here.'

'Any snakes?' Bull said. 'I have this thing about snakes.'

'Relax,' said Pieter. 'I've got everything covered.'

'Apart from why we're here,' I said.

'There is that,' Pieter said, 'but we've been in worse places in the past.'

'That does not fill me with great confidence,' said Bull. 'Any place would be better than Angola, for a start. And Croatia — that was bad — and . . . The list goes on. I'd like to add that I'm a teensy bit uncomfortable around lions.'

'No worries,' said Pieter. 'Chill.'

Give me a gun in my hand, I thought, *and then I might start to chill*.

We went through a gate like in *Jurassic Park*, with high electrified fences, and pulled up outside a clearing. There was a wooden cabin, a large, padlocked building and two outhouses — one large, which was used as a kitchen, judging by the delicious aromas coming out. There seemed to be some Heath Robinson device that functioned as a shower and two blue chemical structures purporting to be what the Americans would call a 'bathroom'. None of it filled me with confidence. On top of the wooden buildings were roofs covered in thatch made from local straw. One hit with something flammable and everything would go up like a rocket.

'Welcome,' said Pieter, as we drew up.

I didn't see a hotel in sight. This was going to be basic to the nth degree.

Stan and Red stood waiting for us. Red was wearing glasses, his eyesight presumably worsening so much that the contact lenses weren't good enough anymore. Stan's hair had more grey since the last time we met. I wondered if it was wishful thinking that we could take on hostile forces anymore.

'The good news is that we have a fridge,' Pieter said.

Wow, that makes all the difference, I thought. Maybe we could chill the enemy to death. Hypothermia, here we come.

Inside was a wooden table, on which there was a reassuring range of guns. I saw the Uzi that I trained on and much loved, and four Kalashnikovs. There was also a shotgun — maybe Pieter had been given some advanced warning from

Red — and a Barrett Monster sniper rifle. It had an effective range of a thousand feet and a bullet that could cut through body armour. A good weapon to have at your disposal.

On a small side table there were five Browning Hi-Power 9mm handguns complete with shoulder holsters. Now was the time I could relax for a little while.

The building just had room for a desk and the small table plus two wicker chairs. There was also a pinboard on one wall with what looked like people's names and days of the week: a roster, perhaps? The room did have the all-important fridge, though. Stan got some beers from inside, popped the tops and handed them around. I have to confess that I liked the beer more than the champagne. Less decadent. Somehow more fitting with the situation. Even more encouraging, I saw two bottles of Polish vodka that Stan must have brought. Everything was looking up now.

Pieter led us outside, where there were six rattan tables with four chairs around each. We dragged up another chair and sat down to watch the sun descend gracefully below the horizon. Always better with a cold beer.

Then it struck me. Where were the tourists?

Pieter caught my look. 'I know what you're thinking. I cancelled this week's safari, hoping we can get the next one running normally after we sort things out.'

'So we have a deadline?' I said.

He nodded. Great news. *Pile on the pressure, Pieter.*

'Here's the story,' he said. 'There have always been poachers around, and my four local rangers and I have been able to deal with them, but in the last few weeks the incidents have spiralled. I suspect one of the rangers is taking payola. The poachers seem to know what our plans are — they're always one step ahead of us. It's a big area to cover. There's a hell of a lot of money to be made from ivory,' he went on. 'Elephant tusks — a hundred thousand pounds for a pair of tusks — are the main target, but I've lost one rhino and there's not many of them alive anymore. They're also after hippo teeth. They're ivory, too.'

'Why is ivory so valuable?' I said. 'It seems like a problem from years past, when sailors carved elaborate designs from the ivory tusks of narwhals. You don't associate it with nowadays.'

'There are two main uses for ivory,' Pieter said. 'Elaborate designs like your years-ago sailors did, and Chinese medicine — it's supposed to clear toxins from the body and give a radiant complexion, something to do with the presence of collagen. It all adds up to a huge demand and high prices. It's possible that you can make ivory synthetically, but it doesn't have key features such as hardness and toughness. Since 1989, the sale of ivory has been banned in many countries under an agreement called CITES, and many other countries joined the list later after elephant populations halved, but that has only driven up prices of natural ivory.'

'How do the poachers get it?' said Bull. 'Do these animals have to die?'

'It is possible to use a stun gun,' said Pieter, 'but it's hard to get in a big enough dose to penetrate an elephant's hide. All my rangers carry a stun gun and a Kalashnikov — that hasn't deterred the poachers. They don't care about anything but the money. They shoot to kill and damn the consequences. Killing a female elephant has the worst result. A baby elephant doesn't mature till twelve years or so. Without a mother, the baby elephant dies too. Two generations wiped out.'

Bull went inside for more beers and to stretch his legs. He came out wearing a shoulder holster with a Browning in the pouch. I could sense his brain ticking. 'What's our next question, Stan?'

'Resources?' said Stan. 'Us and four rangers, one of which may be on the side of the Chinese — it is the Chinese that we are up against, I presume? Anybody else?'

'Just a woman who cooks and cleans, and a young boy who runs errands,' said Pieter. 'It's not a call for the police — they aren't interested. It's a private reserve, and as such we have the responsibility to sort it out. The rangers are good, if we could trust them all. They're used to guiding the tourists around on the open-top bus and the walking safaris.'

'What else?' said Stan.

'Just the armoury you've seen and the stun rifles,' said Pieter. 'We've got the bus and five jeeps, but it's a big area to cover. One last thing. If I don't manage to stop the poachers, the owner has said he'll drop me and bring in someone who can.'

'So it's your future as well as the animals at stake,' I said. 'Anything else to brighten my day?'

'I had a sort of fling with one of the ladies on the last safari, who's got another week in South Africa and said she might drop by.'

'Does "sort of fling" mean what I think?' said Bull. 'Is that what they call a euphemism?'

Pieter nodded.

'I don't suppose she's married,' I said.

'Yes,' said Pieter, 'but not happily so.'

'And that makes all the difference, does it?' Bull said.

'So we have to defend ourselves from an irate husband as well as a bunch of poachers?' Stan was thinking more about the coverage of shooting positions rather than morality.

A tall boy around fourteen or fifteen years came up to announce dinner in ten minutes. He was tall and filling out, wearing a pair of khaki shorts and a blue T-shirt that was too tight for him. Growth spurt?

'That was Ibo,' said Pieter. 'The cook's son. He's a willing lad for any needs. He's smart and the job keeps him under his mother's eye. I imagine you can start to smell the barbecue.'

I smelled meat grilling. Finally, something of which to be glad.

'Are you going to show us the accommodation before dinner?' Red said. 'I'd like to unpack a few things before bedtime.'

'It's not what you would expect,' said Pieter, 'and it's hopefully not for very long.'

My heart sank. This did not bode well. 'Hopefully not for very long' rang alarm bells.

'Follow me,' he said.

'One moment.' Stan's deeply morbid Polish tone sounded even more so than ever. He was not one for optimism. He dealt in realities.

He went into the office and came back with all the guns and holsters and dished them out among us. 'As of now, we always go armed,' he said. 'Can't be too careful. Right, Johnny?'

'I'd say, "Prudence",' I said, 'but Pieter might think it was a lady, and we don't need any further complications.'

Pieter led us behind the office, pointing out the kitchen in one of the sheds and the two blue chemical toilets marked 'Men' and 'Women'. There was a plastic sheet pulled around a shower head with a reservoir over the top which you filled with water from a standpipe. Basic was starting to seem a good deal. There was another clearing with an array of tents.

Oh, God, this was it.

'I thought it would be better if you slept together rather than be separate. Easier to defend.'

How thoughtful.

'And where do you sleep?' I said.

'With you,' he said.

So there were now five of us in the tent that I guessed was built to accommodate two tourists.

'I'm used to tents,' Red said, 'with my Comanche heritage, but isn't this kind of vulnerable? Lions and God knows what else lurking in the shadows.'

'I'll have one of the rangers on patrol through the night,' said Pieter. 'They're used to doing that for the tourists, and I didn't see why you should be treated any worse than them.'

'I hate to say this, Pieter,' I said, 'but people actually pay good money for this?'

'It's communing with nature. A safari like they used to be. No frills. The whole deal built around being up close to the animals. Walking safaris as well as riding in the bus and the jeeps. Camping in the savannah with barbecues and drinks at sundown. Candle lights flickering. Romantic, too — husband and wife brought together in a unique setting.'

I still wasn't convinced. Sounded like money for old rope to me. Maybe Pieter and the owner of the reserve knew what they were doing. Or maybe not.

A stout woman outside the kitchen banged a ladle on an empty saucepan. Dinner was served.

We pulled up another table and lined it up till it turned a square into a rectangle big enough for the plates of five tall men. Pieter went to the shed with the padlock, unlocked it and went inside. He reappeared with five glass tumblers and a bottle of Merlot from the Western Cape. He filled our glasses and I sipped. Pretty good. Everything was looking up.

The charcoal in the barbecue glowed white. There was something that encouragingly looked like steak and some thick sausages in a spiral. A dish of something yellow sat on a low table and we let the woman — Munty, we were told — dish out the goodies.

'So what are we eating?' I asked.

'Springbok,' she said.

'Don't feel bad about it,' said Pieter. 'We have to cull them from time to time or the population rockets. The side dish is chakalaka — cornmeal and spices. The cornmeal is like polenta. The sausages are called boerewors. They are ninety per cent beef. This is the kind of food we serve the tourists, be it here or camping in the bush. Rustic. Enjoy.'

Munty filled my plate and I went back to the table. Red was already digging into his sausage. 'This is good,' he said. 'Not as good as Comanche, of course.'

'What does a Comanche eat?' I said.

'Buffalo.'

'And what if there's no buffalo?'

'We go hungry.'

Ibo picked up another bottle of red wine and topped up our glasses. He looked long and hard at Bull and filled his glass to the brim.

'Do you go to school?' Bull asked.

'No, sir,' Ibo said. 'Too far away. Mama teaches me things.'

'Can you read and write?' said Bull.

'Almost,' said the boy.

Fourteen years old and can't do the basics of human knowledge. I started to wonder if this was going to be a world of two parts — the rich and the poor. No, I chided myself. There are always divisions in any society — as long as there's an opportunity to move from poor to rich, that's what counts. South Africa, from what I read in the papers, had come a long way from the disgraceful days of Apartheid.

'Stick with me tomorrow, boy,' Bull said. 'We'll do some practice.'

The springbok was good. I'd had venison plenty of times back home and this was unsurprisingly similar to a haunch. It had been cooked well — hard to get a barbecue just right — and was still juicy.

'So what's the plan for tomorrow?' I said.

'Some physical training for you, Pieter,' said Bull. 'Unavoidable. Then we can start the rest of the day.'

'We'll take the bus and show you the territory,' said Pieter. 'I'll introduce you to the rangers and take one of them to keep a lookout. He'll have the stun gun and a Kalashnikov for protection. Don't worry about the animals — if we don't bother them, they won't bother us. Like a lot of us, they want a quiet life.'

'I'll take the other stun gun, together with the shotgun. Can't miss an elephant,' Red said.

'I'll start working on some shooting positions in the morning before we go,' Stan put in. 'We've got to be able to defend ourselves here, first of all.'

'I'll take the sniper rifle along with my Uzi, plus the Browning 9mm,' I said. 'Can't ever have too many weapons.'

'Is there a builders close by?' Stan said. 'We can't use the tables as shooting positions — they're too flimsy. A bullet would go through them like a hot knife through butter. I need

24

sand. Best if it could already be in bags. If not, we'll have to get some sacks and fill them ourselves. Waste of our talents.'

'If we cross the builders' palms with enough silver, they'll do that for us,' said Pieter. 'This is beginning to shape up. We're going to crack this. So glad for all of your help. I feel good now.'

'Enough time for a vodka, Stan, before slipping into our cosy tent?' Bull said.

'There's never a time not to have vodka,' said Stan.

I tried to work out the double negative before he smiled and said, 'And I've got a special treat for you.'

In unison, we said, 'Pickled gherkins.'

'How did you know?'

'Just a lucky guess,' I said. 'Now break out the bottle.'

'I'll have one of the rangers outside your tent tonight,' said Pieter. 'Keep a lookout.'

Bull took a sip of the vodka and looked at me. I nodded.

'I'll take first shift,' he said. 'Johnny will take second. Can't be too careful. Hate to put myself at risk when I don't know the calibre of your ranger.'

Red said that he would take third watch and Stan fourth. That left Pieter to slip in to help out whenever he couldn't sleep.

We rolled the vodka round our tongues and sighed. My internal body clock was spinning backwards and forwards from the jet lag and the travel time, effectively losing a day somewhere. Or not. I really didn't know.

I downed the rest of my glass of vodka and stood up. 'Time to turn in. Tomorrow we take short rations. Limit the alcohol. Good night, everyone.'

Bull stood and we walked together to our luxury accommodation. Bull picked up a chair and carried it easily to the front of the tent. A tall man with slim legs, no fat on him, sat outside with a Kalashnikov on his lap and a stun gun on the floor at his right-hand side. We motioned him to stay put rather than getting up.

'Smarfy,' he said, extending his hand.

Bull and I introduced ourselves. Bull collected his assault rifle and made sure his shoulder holster was sitting comfortably. He sat down and I went inside. There were five mattresses, blankets and pillows on the ground and I chose one nearest the entrance. I didn't want anyone to get in the way if there was action.

I dug inside my Bergen and took out camouflage clothes for the following day. I put the Uzi on my right, took off the shoulder holster, placed the Browning under my pillow and set the timer on my watch for two hours. Then I lay down, closed my eyes and drifted off to sleep.

Bang! Bang! Bang!

I snatched up the handgun and leaped up. At the entrance, I peeked out to see if I had to take evasive action from any threat.

It seemed OK. Bull was still sitting in his chair alongside Smarfy.

'Explanation?' I said. 'Why the firing?'

'Snake,' Bull said.

I walked in front of him and saw a snake at his feet. It was in four parts.

'Good shooting,' I said. 'Are you sure it's dead? Don't want to use the whole clip of bullets to make sure?'

'I debated whether to just take his tail off,' said Bull, 'so he could escape and tell all the other snakes to stay away, but I didn't know anything about a snake's brain and how they communicated. Seemed best just to blast it away and up to snake heaven, if there is one.'

I looked at my watch. I had been sleeping for a whole hour. There didn't seem much point going inside for the final hour before my shift. I dragged up another chair and went inside for the Uzi, stun gun and holster for the gun.

'I'll take over,' I said. 'You go inside and get some sleep, if that's possible under the current arrangements. I'll wake Red in three hours' time.'

Bull went inside the tent, followed by Red and Stan, only Pieter to come after doing whatever needed to be done to lock up till the morning. I settled down next to Smarfy. His command of English seemed to be restricted to understanding 'Do this. Do that.' It was going to be a long three hours.

And indeed, that was the case. There was some rustling in the bushes near the campsite, but nothing emerged. I spent the time, while still alert, deciding on the GOAT list of English cricketers, football teams, favourite meals I had had, and so on. I was on favourite locations when Red came out. He tapped me on the shoulder and I rose to hand over the chair.

I managed to sleep for a whole four hours before Stan woke me with a cup of tea. Miracle. You could always rely on Stan.

'All's been quiet,' he said. 'Best to keep our night-time watches as last night as I caught Smarfy about to drop off on a couple of occasions. Eerie place in the dark. You don't know what's lurking. Seems all a bit casual to me, but then I suppose we have to rely on Pieter's knowledge and experience.'

'But you don't like it?'

'It's a bad place to have to defend — there's too little cover. That makes us easy targets. It may be that attack is a better option.'

'Let's take a more detailed view after Pieter gives us the guided tour,' I said. 'Right, let's get this day started.'

I gave Stan my empty cup, thanking him again, and dug into my Bergen for the towel I had packed. It wasn't big, but it would do. I collected my camouflage clothes, toothpaste and shower gel and headed to the makeshift shower I had seen the previous day. If it was good enough for paying customers, I shouldn't complain.

I filled the bucket with water from the standpipe and poured it into the reservoir above the shower head, then stripped off, wrapping the plastic sheet around. I pushed the button and a light rain poured down. I managed to wash and rinse off and was congratulating myself when the sheeting was pulled back and a bucket of water drowned me.

Pieter stood there killing himself with laughter. 'Welcome to South Africa.'

CHAPTER THREE

The bus was what I would have called an open truck with benched seats. It had capacity for twenty people who focused on view rather than comfort. One of the rangers was in the driving seat and another sat in the back with a Kalashnikov and a stun gun. We piled in, kitted up with all our weaponry.

Ibo watched us forlornly. Bull waved to him to jump up and join us. The kid must have thought Christmas had arrived early. He sat up next to Bull and showed his white teeth in a big smile.

The ranger who sat in the back with us was called Ranu, and he was stick thin but strong. He looked like he could run a marathon before breakfast and another one after a couple of fried eggs. He stood up for a better view and I put my trust in him, or maybe some of it. I didn't know how good a shot he was and how he would react in a gunfight involving people and not animals. There were five of us, immodestly speaking, the best shooters in the world, and we could handle any danger. Not that we'd shot any lions before, but past experiences always stood you in good stead. Well, so they say, but I wasn't convinced — it depended on the experience.

Ranu banged twice on the top of the driver's cabin and the bus pulled away and bounced along a well-worn track.

We were clad in our camouflage gear, except for Pieter, who was in his usual uniform of beige shorts and shirt. Our bottles of water and our guns lay on the floor by our sides. I was looking for a chance to fire the sniper rifle, to check the accuracy of its sight, whether it shot high or low, left or right.

It was still only nine o'clock, but the sun was spreading its warmth. The humidity was low, and so not uncomfortable. Savannah surrounded us, seemingly stretching for miles. There was shrubland at its edges and trees beyond that.

Pieter banged once on the driver's cabin. The truck stopped.

'There—' Ibo pointed to one spot in the shrubland — 'Leopard.'

'Leopard at ten o'clock,' shouted Pieter.

Its camouflage worked amazingly well. I strained my eyes in the direction where the boy had pointed and spotted nothing. Then there was a slight movement and I saw it. Majestic. It was slowly creeping behind the shrubs.

'He's waiting for the impalas to start grazing,' said Pieter. 'It will single out a weak one, or maybe one still a baby, and he'll make a dash. Death will be inevitable. Now do you understand why the safaris are so popular?'

I did. There was something about being so close to nature. Communing with it. Electric. The hairs on my arm were standing up. It would be something that would stay with me for ever. It felt as if I understood what life was all about — prey and predator, the law of the jungle. This law involved no judgement of what was good or what was evil, but the way things had to be in order for it all, the ecosystem, to survive. The way of the world.

Where did I and my friends fit in? I couldn't accept that we didn't have a role to play. Were we the ones to be the judges between good and evil? Protecting the weak and keeping the strong in check? I liked to think so.

A group of around a dozen impala came out of the cover of the shrubs to graze. The leopard crouched down. I picked up the sniper rifle and took aim. Two feet to the right of where the leopard lay should do the trick. I steadied the rifle on the top of the driver's cab and let loose a bullet.

The impala scattered. The leopard would go hungry.

The sights were a little high and to the right. I made the adjustment and slipped a bullet into the chamber, ready for next time.

'Why did you do that?' said Pieter. 'The leopard must eat.'

'Granted,' I said, 'but not on my watch.'

Pieter slammed his hand down on the roof of the driver's cabin, partly to tell the driver to move forward, partly as a show of irritation at my action.

'That soft heart of yours will be the death of you one day,' he said.

'And you've grown hard, Pieter. Think of times past and the morality of what we did. We were men of honour. Let honour be your guide.'

I put down the sniper rifle and took up a bottle of water to wet my dry mouth — hands sweat, mouth dries. That's the way it goes when the adrenaline flows.

Ibo looked puzzled.

'Sometimes,' said Bull, 'you don't have to kill. That's a last resort. We can all make a difference. The leopard will make its kill another time, but we didn't have to be a part of it. Maybe there's someone watching us. Maybe that act of kindness will be repaid someday. One can only hope.'

Ibo nodded. Maybe it was the first time he had thought of such a thing. As a boy with what I guessed was a restricted upbringing, he would benefit from such a lesson.

We travelled along for about ten minutes and came to an area of trees surrounding a waterhole. Close by was a group of tents. This must have been an overnight camp for the tourists — a place to watch, over a dry martini, the animals gathering at sundown. In front of the tents, there was a burnt-out patch with half an oil barrel with ashes inside, a spot where you could drink your South African wine and sing songs around the campfire. Or maybe just swap stories. Everybody thrown together and having to interact as strangers. And when they'd all finished their barbecue and drinks and gone to bed, the rangers would take turns to watch out for them.

The watering hole was a place where the laws of existence did not apply. The prey and predator called a truce. Kudus, impala and giraffes drank alongside the cheetahs. We stood there transfixed by the tranquillity of the scene.

'Scenes like this are a once-in-a-lifetime experience,' Pieter said. 'As the saying goes, people will pay good money for this, and there's so much more to come.'

He made to bang his fist on the driver's cab again.

'Not yet,' I said. 'I want to fix every detail of this picture in my mind, so I can remember it for the rest of my life. There are lessons to be learned here.'

'Do you have any trouble here with trophy hunters?' said Red. 'Cougars are still hunted for pleasure in the States. That leopard would look amazing in someone's home. Must be people would go a long way for that head on their wall and the skin on the floor.'

'We deter them through our presence,' said Pieter, 'and we confiscate any guns when they enter the reserve. Seems to work. No trouble with the trophy hunters. It's the poachers we have to worry about.'

'Roll on,' I said. 'What's next?'

'Elephants,' Pieter said. 'Wait till you see one of those up close, in the flesh.'

He banged on the cabin roof and we set off at a sedate speed. I wondered if this was to increase the tension before the big reveal.

Suddenly, with his glasses and Comanche vision, Red shouted, 'Stop! Over there.'

He pointed to a patch of grass. It was stained an iron brown.

Red got out and we followed.

There was a lot of dried blood. A big pool of it had been here. Scattered around were the bodies of three impala.

Red picked up something from the ground and walked back to us. He held out his hand. 'You know what we have got here?'

'Remnants of a hand grenade,' Bull said. 'This takes our job up a notch. I don't like it. There's not much defence against a hand grenade. If you're in the right position, grab it and lob it back. If not, lay flat on the ground and start praying.'

'This is poaching on an industrial scale,' said Pieter. 'See a herd of impala, springbok or whatever, and throw a hand grenade at them. Pick up a few to take home. This scene looks like they got more than they could handle. We must have interrupted them before they could come back and get the rest of their kill.'

'Is this the first time there's been something like this?' I said.

'As far as I know,' said Pieter. 'The lions might have taken any fresh bodies and left the bones. Free meal for them. Hard to spot, unless you were here just after the animals were killed. Any blood would quickly be bleached by the sun.'

'Nothing more to see,' said Red. 'Let's kick on.'

As we travelled along, Ibo chattered away excitedly, pointing out the animals. Ranu, a sour expression on his face, said something to him.

'What did he say?' Bull said.

'He said I was a bad boy. That I wasn't showing respect. That he would tell my mother.'

Bull took a knife from a sheath down an especially designed pocket on his leg. It was a proper commando's knife, one side sharpened and the other side serrated. He tapped the blade on his palm. 'Tell him that if any harm comes to you, I will slice off his balls and feed them to the hyenas.'

Ibo looked aghast.

'Tell him,' said Bull.

Ibo did so. Ranu reeled back and lowered his eyes. He nodded.

'Good man,' said Bull. 'Now where were we?'

About an hour later, the landscape changed into tall trees closer to the savannah. Lurking at the edge, a pack of dogs or something studied us.

Pieter caught my look. 'Wild dogs,' he said. 'They're not really dogs, more like a cross between a smaller version of a wolf and a hyena. They're scavengers, mainly, but will hunt in packs when there isn't any easy meat around.'

'Any danger to your guests?' Bull said. 'They look like trouble to me. Seem pretty curious about us. Do they have a taste for human flesh?'

'They don't bother us while we're on the bus or jeeps. They can get a bit bold at night, due to the smell of the cooking, but when we camp overnight we build a big fire, and that seems to keep them at bay. There's always two of us who keep a watch when it gets dark. One shot and they scatter. Reassures the guests that way. Sometimes we just fire a shot at nothing for that kind of effect.'

A little further on, there were two adult giraffes and a young one nibbling at the leaves of the trees. How they managed to keep their long necks upright seemed an impossibility. They seemed ungainly and yet graceful in equal measure.

Pieter called for a break, for the driver as much as us. We got down and looked around. No bushes to go behind.

Pieter laughed. 'Anywhere you like,' he said. 'It won't make any difference to the animals. They'll just mark out their territory over yours.'

Finished, we drank some water. It was warm and had no refreshment in it. We drank because we had to, to not become dehydrated. I'd have given anything for an ice cube.

We piled back into the truck and motored on for ten minutes or so, and then we saw them.

Elephants. A group of about ten, young and old.

'There's a difference between African and Asian elephants,' said Pieter. 'Female African elephants have tusks, Indian don't. That's why the poachers kill the females as well as the males. We're in the area that we need to protect most.

Elephants love it here. If you look ahead, you'll see that there is a river. Perfect for the elephants — drinking water, as well as a chance to roll over and cool down. There's another of our campsites there. We'll need to use that for lookouts and sleeping.'

'Any protection?' asked Stan. 'Anything to hide behind?'

'Tricky,' said Pieter, which I decoded as a no. Stan was going to hate it. How could one make shooting positions out of nothing? Silk purses out of a sow's ear would be easy in comparison.

We stood there enthralled, watching the elephants in all their majesty. I'd seen them on TV. I'd seen them in the flesh at a zoo. Nothing prepared me for this. With no barriers between the elephants and me, they looked bigger — colossal — and I felt like I could reach out and touch them, pat the thickness of their skin with my fingers, stroke the sensitivity of their trunks and feel those hard tusks with my palms.

Red watched in silence. He seemed to have an affinity with them. While the rest of us were emitting 'oohs' and 'aahs', he jumped down and faced them. He formed his fingers so that each hand had the outside fingers showing and the middle two folded over. He stood there as steady as a rock.

The elephants didn't know what to do. They stood still and watched Red with a casual curiosity, as if deciding whether he was a threat. It was not the best tactic: they could trust us, but that could increase their vulnerability to the poachers. It may sound silly, but I felt that they were communicating among themselves, taking a collective view of us. They must have been used to the bus with the regular visits from the tourists. I wanted to clap my hands and make them scatter, drive them away. As a herd, they were too easy a target.

'Don't get any closer,' said Pieter. 'The females will be protective of the young ones. The males look after the whole herd and may charge if they feel threatened.'

Ranu shouted at Pieter.

'Poachers!' Pieter said.

Red darted back.

Up ahead, there was a swirl of dust as the poachers' jeep started a manoeuvre to turn around. There was no way that our bus could catch them up. I picked up the sniper rifle, steadied it, took aim and let fly a bullet.

Bingo!

The rear wheel on the right-hand side erupted and the jeep tilted over.

'I think we have just registered our intent,' I said.

* * *

There was no wildlife at the river. Pieter said that the animals avoided the full heat of the day, or maybe they had been warned off by the noise of the poachers' jeep or my shot. There was, however, the decapitated body of a kudu, a kind of antelope where the males have large and elaborately curled horns. This was a trophy kill while the poachers waited for the elephants to arrive — they respected no life. The carcass was already being savaged by a pack of wild dogs ripping chunks out of it. Bodies were not left for long before the scavengers took their prize.

We got down from the bus and splashed our faces with the water, providing some relief from the heat. The encampment — a collection of tents, a marquee with the sides rolled up, and, as before, a firepit made from an oil-drum — was set back from the river, but close enough to give a clear view for the tourists. We went inside one of the tents, leaving Ranu and the driver, Ackta, on guard smoking their roll-ups. Ackta was a short man, and from his height, I guessed he was not of Zulu origin.

We sat down in a rough circle in the shade. There was a leather bucket in one corner. I picked it up and gave it to Ibo. 'Fetch some water, please, Ibo.'

He happily picked up the bucket, glad to be playing a part in our journey, and went out of the tent.

'Right,' I said, 'a note of caution. If you are right, Pieter, that there is a viper in the nest, we need to be more guarded. None of our plans should be revealed until the very last minute. No rota on your pinboard for starters. That includes Ibo. I suspect that none of us thinks he is the traitor, but he might let slip something that we've said. Tight lips from now on.'

'How much more is there to see?' Stan said.

'Another hour's worth or so,' said Pieter.

'More elephants?' I said.

'We've seen the two main sites now. There might be some stragglers from the herd, but that's about it.'

'Here is where we must wait,' said Stan. 'We can't split our forces by covering both places — not enough of us. To get to the first place we saw, the poachers will presumably stick to the track and have to come past here. We can throw them off the scent if we light a fire at the first place. If we come here by bus, then we give away our position and the poachers can simply wait us out — we can't act as guards for ever. We need to park back at the first site and then come here by foot. A fire would be risky in this parched country, so someone needs to be stationed there.'

'It's a hard place to defend,' Red said. 'The trees give us a bit of cover, but then we might be vulnerable to being pinned down. Maybe we'd be better off attacking rather than defending. Catch them off guard.'

'Where are the poachers coming from?' I said. 'Where is their base?'

'There are two villages near here,' said Pieter. 'I suspect it's one of those.'

'Then we scout them out,' I said. 'I like Red's idea about attack rather than defence. Something we should consider.'

Ibo came back and brought me the bucket. I washed my hands and passed it round for others to do the same.

'Where do we go from here?' Stan said. 'Just a hint will do. I don't need to know the details.'

'We'll drive on for another hour until we get to the northern boundary that marks our territory from the next private reserve,' Pieter said. 'You'll have seen a good deal of the territory then. The mountains look good in this light. We can cover the rest another time. The guests have got the week, so plenty of time for them to see the animals.'

There was a problem with the northern boundary. This was where the poachers came and went. The fence had been cut and pulled aside so that a jeep could pass through. That would need to be restored — couldn't have poachers coming in and animals going out.

We picked up our weapons and exited the tent. Ackta was already in his cabin and Ranu was standing waiting for us. We climbed aboard and after giving the signal, we motored on.

We got our first sight of a white rhino. Frightening. It was grazing the other side of the trees. This was a serious animal. It radiated strength. The two horns looked like they could disembowel you with one flick.

The white rhino weighs in around two thousand kilograms, the male being larger than the female. That's about two tons in old money. Imagine that charging at you. Brutal.

Pieter told us it was now endangered. So sad, and all because of the allure of ivory.

The mountains were dramatic after the low flatlands of the savannah. The sun was beginning to sink behind them and its shadows were lengthening. We would soon be turning back while it was still light.

The day had changed me. I would never be the same again. I felt awe, I felt respect, I had love for these humbling creatures.

CHAPTER FOUR

We sat drinking beers and watching the sun go down in silence.

Finally, Pieter spoke. 'Now do you understand? Now do you see why I have changed? I feel so insignificant compared to what is all around me. I feel powerless.'

'Well, you'd better change back before you're supposed to be protecting me on my right flank,' I said.

'Or me on my left,' said Bull. 'It seems to me you have an important job here. Without you, the poachers would run riot. You need to regain your perspective and your confidence. When was the last time you had an exercise regime? When was the last time you had gun practice? You have grown sloppy, Pieter. You need to change back, and to do it quickly. Otherwise, you're a liability, and I'm out of here.'

A Land Rover pulled into the camp and a short, fat man got out. He had grey hair and a red face and I suspected he looked older than his age, which I put as fifty going on sixty. He was wearing khaki chinos and a light-blue short-sleeved shirt. His tan loafers looked out of place in the dust of the camp.

'The owner,' Pieter said. 'Van Lloyd. Be on best behaviour.'

'So this is what you do all day, is it? Sit in the shade drinking beer while someone is poaching my elephants?'

'Pleased to meet you, Mr Van Lloyd,' I said. 'I'd like to point out that we've been eating dust all day, travelling your reserve. The sun's going down, and so night is falling. I bet the poachers are doing pretty much the same as us. Let's start again. Can I get you a beer? Be rude not to.'

He gave a grunt and nodded. I called Ibo over and told him what I wanted. He came back and handed the beer to Van Lloyd and the cardboard drip mats to me. I counted the top five from the pile and handed them back to him, then told him to place them in the branches of a tree about twenty yards away.

Bull gave a smile. He knew what I had planned. It was an old stunt, but worth another outing. Might be the only laugh we got with Mr Van Lloyd.

'Let me show you something.' I pulled out the Browning from its holster and let off a bullet. The farthest beer mat was gone in a flash.

'Bull?'

Bull took out his gun and blew away the second beer mat.

I nodded at Stan and he disposed of another.

'Time for you, Pieter,' I said. 'Don't mess up.'

Pieter seemed to take an age while he got another beer mat in his sights.

He did it! Another drip mat shattered. Only one left.

'OK, Red,' I said. 'Show the man what you can do.'

Red picked up his shotgun and fired. Half the tree went with the last drip mat.

'There's one more trick,' I said. 'Shall we do it, Bull?'

'Be a shame not to.' He got up and placed a beer mat in a branch not blown away by Red's shotgun. He stood back and admired his handiwork, or something like that. 'Over here, Johnny.'

I got up and stood directly in front of him, closed my eyes and raised the gun in what I thought was about the right place.

'How many bullets do you have left. Five?' he said.

I moved the gun to the left. Five degrees.

'You're going to feel high around two o'clock if you get this.'

I raised the gun higher.

'Shoot,' said Bull.

I fired, and from the gasp from Van Lloyd I knew that I had hit the target — thanks to Bull's directions. I walked back to my seat, Bull following me, and I took a pull of my beer.

'If you had any doubts about what we can do, Mr Van Lloyd,' I said, 'I hope we've dispelled them. The poachers won't stand a chance when we track them down.'

'Impressive,' he said. 'Makes my mind up. I'm not cancelling next week's safari.'

'What!' said Pieter. 'You can't. There are men out there with rifles trained on elephants. High-velocity bullets, if I sense right, that shatter an elephant's skull. Do you want people to remember this holiday as the day they saw an elephant shot down?'

'I want some money in the bank,' he said. 'They will have a good time. I trust Pieter for that. Drinks, barbecues, sat around the campfire singing before they give in, a little unsteady, and wake early for the next day's drive, adrenaline coursing through their brains, and a need for a couple of paracetamols.'

'Having tourists around is not part of our game plan,' said Stan.

'Well, you'd better come up with a new one,' Van Lloyd said. 'I can't fund the upkeep of this reserve without the income from the tourists. I am not made of money. There is no magic money tree for me to pick from. Like it or not, my mind is made up.'

'Maybe if we don't do the night camps that might decrease the need for protection,' said Stan.

'The night camps stay,' Van Lloyd said. 'They're part of the deal, part of the experience, and you said the poachers won't work at night. I don't see them being a problem.' He drained his beer and called across at Ibo. 'Fetch me another beer, boy,' he said. 'Make it snappy.'

I felt Bull bristle. 'You know,' he said, 'in life, I've found a "please" helps to get things more quickly. His name is Ibo. You might try using that the next time you want something.'

'You may be able to shoot a few beer mats,' Van Lloyd said, 'but that doesn't entitle you to act as my moral guardian. This is my business, my country, and I'll call him whatever I like.'

'Let's you and I go for a walk.' I rose from my chair and placed my hand on Bull's arm. We left the table together and walked fifty yards away to the tented camp.

'Don't let him get to you. He's a stubborn pig, and whatever we do, he'll always be a stubborn pig. I've seen you angry many times, and I don't want to have to scrape him off the floor and put the bits back together. Bad for business. Bad for Pieter.'

'Do you reckon Pieter can get his act together before the fighting starts?' Bull said.

'He shot the drip mat.'

'Took a long time to aim,' Bull said. 'That could be the difference between life and death.'

'Take him through one of your sessions tomorrow. Run, press-ups, shooting practice. Make him sweat. Make him feel good about his progress. Like he's getting his life together again.'

'I kinda get where he's coming from,' Bull said. 'Hard not to doubt yourself when there's so much wonder going on around you. That rhino! Blows you away.'

'Majestic,' I said. 'I'd hate to see it shot for the sake of its horns.'

'I wonder if we're acting too defensively. A bit more offensive would be good. Let's get proactive. My trigger finger is getting itchy, and I've got nothing to aim at.'

'We hit the road tomorrow and see what we can find,' I said. 'Be good if the sandbags come, too. I know it's defensive, but I'll feel safer with some shooting positions built. If we create enough problems for the poachers, we might force them to shoot at us, rather than the elephants and rhino.'

'Are we going to kill them?' Bull said. 'Or just play patsy?'

'Play hardball,' I said. 'We'll kill them if we have to. If that's the only option open to us, we will shoot to kill. My conscience will be clear, judging from what we saw of the animals. They'll not hesitate to kill us, so we'll get our retaliation in first.'

'I like it,' said Bull. 'Back to Mr Pig.'

We walked back to the table and took our places. Van Lloyd was still there, unfortunately, but Bull said he'd keep his mouth shut unless it was open for drinking his beer.

Van Lloyd couldn't stop getting under my skin. 'You know I'm not going to pay you for this?' he said.

'We never doubted it,' I said. 'We're not here for the money.'

'Then why are you here?' he said.

'It's something called friendship,' I said. 'You could do with a dose or two. It's coupled with honour. How you live and interact with others. If you follow the code, you will never be ashamed.'

'Hah.'

Brilliant response. Who could answer to that?

'If we all had honour,' I said, 'think what a difference it would make to humankind. A promise is a promise, and must be kept. Pieter saved my life a while ago. And "a while ago" makes no difference. Yesterday or ten years past, we have to act with honour.'

'Sounds like a code to get yourself killed,' he said. 'There's no honour in that.'

'To give up your life to save another will be the ultimate sacrifice,' I said. 'You don't need a medal to say you did the right thing. You'll always be there in someone's heart.'

'And who's to judge? Who's going to make me account-able? The grim reaper?' He laughed.

'I'd like to take a bet on Bull putting a bullet between your eyes,' I said.

'And that would serve honour?'

'And give one a warm feeling, too,' I said.

'I'll vouch for that,' said Bull. 'Without a moment's hesitation.'

Van Lloyd laughed again. 'You guys are living in the wrong century. This isn't a scene from the Wild West. You're dinosaurs. They died out years ago. Get real.'

'I'd hate to think that some girlband said it all,' I said, 'but they got it right when they said friendship never ends.'

'Humbug.'

Perfect Scrooge impersonation. What can you do with a man like that? Take him away, would seem an appropriate answer, but would we ever get the chance?

He stood up from the table. 'Some of us have got work to do. I'll send some boys along to help with getting everything set up for the arrival of the guests. Don't mess this up, Pieter, or I'll be forced to look around for someone else. Regard this as being on borrowed time. Shouldn't be difficult to find someone who'd like to have a cushy job like this, driving around all day like the lord of the manor.'

He left just before Bull totally lost control and rearranged the man's head to point backwards. Van Lloyd didn't know how lucky he was.

Unasked, Ibo brought more beers. He handed Bull a bottle. 'Thank you.'

'There's a lesson here, Ibo,' Bull said. 'You will meet many people like Van Lloyd in your life. Men like him enjoy throwing their weight around. In those cases, you have to forget your pride and take it on the chin. Sometimes you will get an opportunity to take them down a peg, but not frequently. When that time comes, relish the moment when it will be you giving the lessons. Don't get carried away. If you succeed, don't fall into the trap of becoming like them. Treat others as you would expect to be treated. Then you won't go far wrong.' He took a swig of his beer. 'Come and sit with us for a while.'

'Let me get you a drink, Ibo,' I said. 'What would you like?'

Ibo looked at Pieter for his approval. Pieter nodded, and Ibo sat down. 'May I have a juice, please, sir?' he said to me. 'Any juice, please.'

I went to the fridge and took out a carton of orange juice and poured some into a proper glass like the tourists used, took it back and handed it to Ibo.

'What do you want to do when you grow up, Ibo?' said Bull.

'I want to be a ranger, sir,' he said. 'To look after the animals. I love the animals. If I could be a ranger, I would be very happy. My mother would be happy, too. I think she doesn't know what to do with me.'

'To be a ranger, you would need properly to learn reading and writing and your numbers,' I said. 'You will have to work hard.'

'I would do that, sir.'

Bull looked at Pieter. 'Can you arrange for some lessons?'

'There is a retired teacher in one of the villages,' Pieter said. 'I am sure she would love to take on the task. She would do it for love, but we'll pay her for her trouble. There's something I can do too. How would you like to go out with the rangers? Learn what they do. It would be like an apprenticeship — learning on the job.'

'I would be most honoured, sir,' Ibo said.

'I could draw up a schedule,' said Stan. 'A simple spreadsheet with the area to be covered.'

'Then it shall be done,' said Pieter. 'For now, Ibo, find out how soon dinner will be. We're all starving.'

Ibo drained his glass and went off.

'You've met Van Lloyd,' said Pieter. 'Now you see what I have to put up with.'

'Can't be easy,' said Red. 'In Texas, we have oil barons that act like that, throwing their weight around. They think they own everything and can order people around.'

'And what do you do?'

'Grin and bear it. The Comanches might go to the medicine man and get him to put a spell on such a man.'

'I hate to say this,' I said, 'but does it work?'

'No,' said Red. 'Apart from for the medicine man, that is, because he pockets the money for the spell.'

I screwed up my eyes. 'I'm finding it hard to understand the moral behind this story.'

'Just thought it might be interesting. Relevant in some way. You know? You can learn a lot from the Comanches.'

'Thank you for your contribution,' said Bull. 'Always good to have a Comanche in the tent revealing the wisdom of an old culture.'

'I still don't get it,' said Stan.

'Just think of it as how would Poland be without pickled gherkins,' I said.

'Ah,' he said. 'That all makes sense now.'

Best to move on, I thought, while I was ahead. 'Where's that barbecue? I'm getting worried that I can't smell anything.'

The sound of the saucepan being gonged arrived just in time, before the conversation got into *Alice in Wonderland* territory, in which everything had a coded meaning. Let's not go down that rabbit hole yet, I thought.

We queued up and saw a casserole dish filled with something Pieter told us was called bobotie, another of the national dishes of South Africa. It was a little like a moussaka, minced beef with an eggy topping. Munty served us portions, and we regarded our plates as though they contained another of life's mysteries. The decision not to have some barbecued meat was a brave one.

It was good. We breathed a sigh of relief and ate hungrily. No wine tonight — we had to keep alert at all times now. A few beers didn't come into the equation. Maybe a shot of vodka, though. Just the one. Savour it.

'Plans for tomorrow, Johnny?' said Stan.

'The sandbags are due to come in the morning,' said Pieter. 'Might have to tailor what we do around that.'

'I want Pieter to show me the two villages that might harbour our poachers,' I said. 'I'd like Stan to organise the defences, with Bull and Red helping. Stan, I want the firing positions like trenches, with sandbags fore and aft, in case the attack comes from the rear. We ought to think of some kind of stockade for the visitors to shelter in. Pieter and I will pitch in with construction when we arrive back from our travels. Pieter, set Ibo out with one of your rangers. Purely observation, no guns for him. He'll have to do that someday, but he needs to learn when to shoot and when not. That will be in a few years' time. Stretch him. He's a bright lad, and could be very useful when he's trained. He's an uncut diamond at the moment. He needs to be fashioned and polished in the time to come.'

Red went back for another helping, and it seemed like a good idea. When we were back at the table, the inevitable question was posed.

'What about the guests?' Bull said. 'We didn't factor that in. A stockade is a good idea if we have sufficient warning of an attack. We can't have them wandering about. One of us will need to marshal the defence of the stockade, too. That weakens our position here.'

'When are they due to arrive?' I said to Pieter.

'Two days' time,' Pieter said.

'Two days!' said Red. 'What the hell can we do in two days?'

'We make this place our last refuge in case of attack,' I said.

'It may be something evident that I've missed, but why don't we call in the police or the army?' said Red.

'Because they can't be here all the time,' I said. 'If we call in reinforcements, the poachers will simply wait until the budget runs out and then start up again. We have to defeat them. Get rid of them for good. Sun Tzu said in the classic book *The Art of War* that to win a battle you have to defeat an enemy's best troops. That's what we will do. If they don't come to us, we will go to them.'

'Hallelujah, brother,' said Bull. 'Bring it on.'

46

CHAPTER FIVE

Stan brought me a cup of tea at dawn. There must have been something about to happen that warranted waking me at such an ungodly hour, but that's life as a mercenary for you.

Crawling out of the tent, I saw Pieter in a pair of shorts and a vest, and Bull shouting at him to get a move on. Both had shoulder holsters on. Take no chances, obviously. The daily ritual: running and press-ups. I didn't want to miss this. I changed into a pair of boxer shorts, no top. It would get hot soon once the sun was fully up. I didn't know how long the run would be, but it had to be a fair bit of time to make the early start necessary.

We set off. The pace wasn't great because of Bull's hamstrung leg. Slow, but Bull could keep it up all day. We followed the track that we had driven down in the truck the previous day. A giraffe watched us with what I took to be a bemused expression on its face. I might have been wrong — giraffes can be inscrutable.

At first, Pieter had no problem, but after about a mile he started to falter and his breathing got more laboured. The second mile was worse.

'Pick up the pace, guys,' Bull shouted.

I ran alongside Pieter and told him he could do it. 'Make an effort. Not long to go,' I said, although I had no idea if that was true.

A herd of impalas seemed like they might join us to find out what this new phenomenon was but decided they'd continue to graze while the predators were still sleeping. Lions and leopards — I've never shot one before, and I sure didn't want to start now.

There's an old story about two hikers coming across a lion. One hiker takes a pair of spiked running shoes out of his backpack and starts putting them on. The other hiker tells him that's silly, that he wouldn't be able to outrun the lion, even with spiked shoes. The first man says he doesn't have to outrun the lion: 'I only have to outrun you.'

The savannah was a good surface for running, short grass above springy earth. We ran on for another mile, and Pieter had to finally give up — on the way forward, that is, still the run home to tackle.

'One minute rest,' said Bull, 'then we head back for press-ups.'

Pieter groaned at the prospect. He put his hands on his knees and leaned forward, breathing hard.

Bull assessed the situation. 'You've made a good start. Maybe we'll just walk back and see how you get on.'

'I didn't realise how out of condition I'd become,' said Pieter.

'We may need to run from the first camp and the second,' I said. 'Remember, we won't have the truck or a jeep, as they're so easily spotted. You need to cover that distance quickly. I'd suggest another run just before sunset. I realise this might be a pain, but it's less so than a bullet thudding into you.'

'OK,' he panted, 'I appreciate what you're trying to do. Let's compromise and jog the whole way back rather than running.'

And so we jogged back.

The giraffe looked at us as if to say, 'I told you so.'

* * *

48

Once back, I showered and changed into my normal camouflage trousers, a T-shirt and a loose-fitting jacket. I knew it would get hot soon, but I needed the jacket to hide the Browning in the shoulder holster and the trousers to disguise my commando knife. It was an odd outfit, and I wouldn't qualify for the most-stylish-person awards. But needs must. Who cared?

Pieter was half dead when we set off, grateful to be in the driver's seat, or any seat come to that.

There were two possible towns — some of the buildings simply mud huts — in which the poachers had made their centre of operations, one to the east of our reserve and one to the north. I favoured the north, because it provided more distance to us and a quicker response to any warning to that fence. It might give us the edge.

We hadn't gone more than ten miles when we had the breakthrough. There were a few basic shops — butcher, baker, pharmacy and so on. But there was also a garage. On the forecourt was a jeep with a jack under the back tyre on the driver's side. Johnny Silver, take a bow.

'Stop! Stop! Stop!' I shouted.

Pieter skidded to a halt.

'Well,' I said, 'we now know where the poachers get their jeeps fixed. We only now need to find out the location of their HQ. Go inside and pretend that we are looking for another jeep. Would the owner be willing to sell? How do we make contact? I'll just be behind, doing what needs to be done. Understand?'

We parked up and strolled — non-suspiciously, I hoped — to the garage forecourt. It was no more than two buildings knocked together with additions like the pit for working below a car. Two people were inside doing esoteric things under the bonnet of an aging Mercedes.

While Pieter played his role of getting attention and information, I looked at the jacked-up tyre. Brand new. What a shame. I took out my commando knife and dug it deep inside the tyre, then walked nonchalantly back to our jeep and waited for Pieter.

'They didn't know whether the owner would sell the car,' said Pieter, 'but gave me his address. It's a building to the north of town. Been unoccupied for a while, and the residents don't come to town much — keep out of the way, it seems. Now for the interesting part — they're Chinese.'

'Aha,' I said. 'Sounds like they want to cut out the middleman. Source the ivory themselves via the poaching, and then straight back to China. A bit audacious — they stand out like a sore thumb around here. Did the garage say anything else?'

'Only that they pay their bills quickly, and this is one of four jeeps they have, which are old and require regular maintenance. Valued customers.'

'Let's take a trip, then, and see their hideaway.'

'Tally-ho,' said Pieter. And we drove away.

Pieter told me that the towns around here had been affected by a bypass when the visitor numbers grew and that there wasn't much trade anymore. They'd become ghost towns, effectively. Poverty was high, and the locals would do anything to earn a dollar. That would make it easy to recruit willing workers — a bit of poaching must seem like steady work to them. I wondered if the local men would be used as cannon fodder by the Chinese in any move we made against them. Slaughter without caring.

We motored on for a few miles along roads that hadn't been repaired since the bypass was built. There were potholes, some deep, and cracks in the surface. A jeep was the ideal vehicle if you wanted to get around.

The HQ of the Chinese was a two-storey house surrounded by a high wall with barbed wire on the top. The barbed wire looked shiny and new, and I guessed that it had been added by the current occupants. Entry was by a double gate wide enough for vehicles to pass through easily. The gate was padlocked.

The high walls would be a liability in an attack, since they hid any activity outside. I heard dogs barking, which didn't please me. We would have to find a way of subduing them. I didn't want to shoot them — how can one protect wild animals and then finish up killing dogs? It was not only against my principles but the sound of firing could alert those inside. Conundrum.

Pieter and I got out of the jeep and walked around the perimeter looking for any weak points. At places, there were parts of an original wall — these were fabricated out of dried mud. I got out my commando knife, dug it into the wall and worked the serrated edge of the knife around. It went in easily, but would take a while to make a hole big enough to let a man pass through.

I looked through the hole I had made and saw three jeeps parked at the back of the house, giving them the four in total. Good news. If they were here, then they weren't at the reserve. Maybe they were puzzled by my shooting of the tyre — what was going on? It had bought us a bit more time to organise ourselves. Stan would be pleased.

We got back into the jeep, and I asked Pieter where Van Lloyd lived. Ten miles away. Out of curiosity, I asked to take a look at it.

It was a ranch rather than a single building. There were cattle in a field surrounded by an electric fence similar to that at the reserve. Always a demand for beef in South Africa, Pieter said.

The building itself was a three-storey house comprising a middle section and two wings, so that the site looked like an H. Why the need for such a large place? He might have live-in staff, workers for the cattle and so on, but it would take a lot to fill such a building. For show? Pure arrogance? I went for the latter, with a dash of the former.

For such a fine place, it was not protected very well. There was one person at the gate, and no visible sight of anyone else. Maybe there were more around the back, but I hadn't seen anyone through my peephole. More likely, he was a Scrooge all the way — watching every penny and cutting everything back to the bone. Strange how some wealthy people are so parsimonious. How they got to be wealthy, I suppose.

We had been out too long, considering how much work there was to do at the reserve. We motored back and found a hive of industry. Stan had everything organised as usual. A driver and his mate were unloading a builder's lorry piled high with sandbags. Everyone was lined up at the back of the truck transporting sandbags as fast as they were unloaded. The shooting positions were in an advanced state, but the work on the stockade for the visitors had not started. This would be the biggest of our defences and needed to be tall — the shooting positions were low, designed for lying down. It was going to take a lot of fortifying. I stripped off the jacket and T-shirt and sought out Stan.

'Too slow,' he said. 'The rangers are doing their usual rounds of the reserve. That means it's down to the five of us to do the work. Ibo volunteered. He's a good kid. He's chipping in, but he can't carry anywhere near to us grown men.'

'Where would you like us?' I already knew the answer.

'The stockade.'

Got it.

'I'll feel happier once we make progress there,' Stan went on. 'How did you guys get on?'

'We managed to destroy their brand-new tyre, thanks to a commando's knife and a bit of skullduggery. We found their base, too. I'd like you to take a look when you have a spare moment — it needs your tactical genius,' I said. 'I thought of something else we need — some easy form of communication between everybody. It's a big place, and we need to know what the position is around the reserve. I don't want to arrive at a place where there is no signal for my mobile.'

'Oh, ye of little faith,' Stan said. 'When have I let you down? I've sourced some walkie-talkies though the internet, and they will be delivered by the end of the day. I've also lined up a comms handler so that the five of us are free. His name is . . . Ibo! I don't expect a round of applause, but a cold beer would be good.'

'Coming up,' Pieter said.

Stan waited until he was out of earshot. 'How did he do this morning?'

'He's way out of shape, but he realises that now and is giving it his all. It's the best we can do. When we choose the formation for moving from the first camp to the second, I'd suggest putting him in the front. Give him a head start.'

Pieter arrived back with some beers and distributed them to us, giving us the break we all deserved.

'You seem to have everything here under control with the shooting positions,' I said to Stan. 'How about Pieter and I finish our beers and get started straightaway on work on the stockade?'

'Offer gratefully received,' he said. 'When everything is unloaded from the builder's truck, I'll pay them some money to help you. I don't foresee that they would refuse. Once we've done here, we need to rebuild the fence to the north where the poachers have been coming through. Won't cause them much trouble — they'll simply cut through again — but it will save us a little time and signal that there's someone watching out. It will stop any animals escaping, too. So much to do, so little time.'

Pieter and I finished our beers and began work. We started by putting four sandbags at the corners of what we saw as the perimeter of the stockade. We had to build sufficient protection for twenty people, and we made a guess about how big it should be. Once we had our basic dimensions set out, there was the heavy work to do. Pieter would be made to sweat again, which would be good for his fitness regime.

We got a system going that halved the walking. I took four bags, the most one person could carry, to the middle of the distance between us and Pieter carried them to the stockade and set them down. It was a backbreaking procedure, and it was a relief when we heard Munty bang a saucepan.

She had laid on beef — what else? — sandwiches with a salad of sliced vegetables. We devoured the sandwiches and ate the vegetables because we didn't want to offend her. She had a lot to learn about the mercenary diet. One beer was allowed by Stan as the maximum we could have until the work was done.

Slowly, things took shape. Stan lay down in the shooting positions to check their height and declared himself satisfied. That released everybody to move on to the stockade. My only worry was how we could sell all these fortifications to the guests without making them paranoid. If we had them here, we might as well still make their stay enjoyable.

We finished about half an hour before sundown, took showers and collapsed on the chairs at our extended table. We raised the bottles, toasted one another for the good work done and awaited the dinner gong to ease our rumbling stomachs. Bull let Pieter off his evening run, and all was jolly, despite aching muscles.

Munty had laid on another first for us in our adventure of South African food — bunny chow, although, thankfully, there was no bunny in it. It consisted of a hollowed-out loaf of bread filled with a beef curry. Good, hearty fare, ideal for those who had been straining every sinew during the day.

'What do you serve the guests?' I asked Pieter. 'Everything anglicised?'

'We do tone things down a notch, but basically what Munty has been serving us. Preponderance of beef and boerewors, some in curries like tonight, but mostly barbecues. Munty prepares everything in advance and the rangers finish it off when they arrive at the camps. Otherwise, she serves everything here. Informal seating at these tables, guests mixing in with one another. We tend to find a camaraderie develops among them. They mingle well as the safari progresses. Relationships are forged.'

'I've been thinking about what we tell the guests,' I said. 'I have a passable explanation. What if we say that we have agreed to be part of an army training exercise? We'll be around and have to carry weapons for the purposes of realism. We'll try to minimise any disruption, but may pop up from time to time. It's a bit lame, but the best I could think of.'

'It's a bit like calling the A-Team "Neighbourhood Watch",' said Red, 'but I'd be happy to go with that. I could tell some of my Comanche stories around the campfire to entertain them. The one about Manitou giving the lands to the tribes would go down well.'

'Nice idea,' Bull said, 'but they might be too tired. Maybe we could keep that in reserve, if conversation lags?'

'We have a plan,' I said.

'We always have a plan,' said Stan, 'but sometimes the plan isn't very good.'

CHAPTER SIX

The giraffe wasn't there this morning. Maybe it had had enough amusement for one week. We three pounded along the track and Peter seemed to be coping better, or was that just wishful thinking?

I knew Stan would have the day mapped out, but it couldn't hurt for me to make my own task list, in the rare case that he had forgotten anything. The fence needed to be fixed for the sake of escaping animals, and to make life just that little bit harder for the poachers. Then there were shooting positions needing construction at the two overnight camps — we would need more sandbags for that — and checking everything for the imminent arrival of the guests. We'd been lucky so far that the poachers had stayed away, but that wouldn't last. I cursed Van Lloyd for putting the guests at risk for the sake of a bundle of money, when, judging by his house, he had plenty in the kitty. My curse, however, wasn't going to affect anything. We had to get used to the complication and do the best we could.

We arrived back and I showered while Bull was taking Pieter through the press-up stage of his rehabilitation, and then I met a new face — the last of the rangers. His name was

Banti. He was short, overweight and had tribal scars under his eyes. He had a menacing air. You wouldn't want to meet him on a dark night. He didn't talk much, and when he did, it was punctuated by grunts before and after. Still, he must have known his job, otherwise he wouldn't have been on the payroll. Frankly, I couldn't have stood for that attitude.

A jeep arrived with three people inside — the promised help by Van Lloyd in terms of getting all the tents checked and everything else for the arrival of the guests. They were taken aback by all the fortifications in the camp. They checked guy ropes and groundsheets until they were happy with the result and topped up the water barrel. When they had finished, Stan told them to get ready to check everything at the first camp.

Pieter and Bull showered, and everybody was ready listen to Stan's orders of the day. Before he started, Pieter took me aside and into the office.

'I have something to show you.' He unlocked the gun rack and took out a brute of a rifle. 'It's something I've never used and hope never to. It might come in handy, though.'

He passed the gun to me. It was very long, very thick and very heavy — in fact, any *very* you could think of.

'It's a .458 elephant gun.' Pieter said. 'The early models were smoothed barrels: this one is later and spiralled for greater accuracy. Which isn't of much relevance — the target you would be aiming at is the elephant's head — too big to miss. One bullet this size blows its brains out. I suspect the poachers have one of these, judging by the wounds found on the dead elephants. We might as well have one, too.'

'I'll give this to Red,' I said. 'I already have the Uzi and the sniper rifle to carry. Even with Red's deteriorating eyesight, he wouldn't miss with this. His new glasses seem to have worked well, judging by him being the first to spot the dried blood on the savannah.'

Pieter displayed a second weapon. 'This is a dart gun. No sense in killing a lion when you can put it to sleep.'

The briefing started.

'Pieter,' said Stan, 'which is the jeep you can afford to lose most?'

'Ranu's one,' Pieter said. 'It's the most unreliable.'

'Good. We're going to use that to block the hole in the fence until we can repair it. Park it sideways and take out the carburettor, so it can't be hotwired and driven off. The only ways out of that are to lift it manually or to push it with another jeep. You can get one of the rangers to set off now.'

Pieter told Ranu to set off, and it was then back to Stan.

'Van Lloyd's men can start to check the facilities at the first camp and wait for more sandbags to arrive to fortify it with shooting positions. Make sure there's a big fire ready to be lit for the guests' first night. Once we're happy with the first camp, we'll move on to the second.'

Van Lloyd's helpers set off, and we were reduced to the five of us, and Ibo, of course.

'We need to check out the comms system,' Stan said. 'Ibo will be here at the base camp in charge of the system. If anything happens here, Ibo will broadcast the information to all of us. Otherwise, communications will be between the five of us. If any walkie-talkie goes down, Ibo will call that through, so that one of the rest of us can investigate.

'When we form up,' Stan continued, 'Pieter will take pole position — front centre — Johnny, front right, Bull, front left and Red and I will take the rear flanks. Red will carry the elephant gun and his shotgun, Johnny his Uzi and the sniper rifle. Pieter will carry the dart gun, and the rest of us will take the Kalashnikovs. All of us will wear the Brownings all the time. It's an awkward load, but we've managed that before, so no grumbles. Red and Pieter will go in one jeep driven by Ranu, together with Ackta. The rest of us will go in another jeep driven by Banti. Ibo will sort out the transport of the sandbags. Happy, Ibo?'

'Yes, sir,' Ibo said. 'I am honoured.'

'If there's any trouble, Ibo,' Stan said, 'don't be a hero. Contact us and we'll respond. Test the equipment every fifteen minutes. Any questions?'

'Shoot to kill or shoot to cripple?' said Red.

'Johnny?' said Stan.

'We'll start off by shoot to cripple. Disrupt their logistics, too — tyres, driver's windscreen, that sort of thing. Watch how they act and respond to us. If they shoot to kill, then so will we.'

A saucepan sounded.

'We can't go on an empty stomach,' said Stan. 'I asked Munty to fry some eggs. We'll test the walkie-talkies while we eat.'

I didn't know how she did it, but Munty fried ten eggs, each perfectly cooked with runny yolks and added two thick slices of bread to our plates. No one asked for ketchup — we may be mercenaries, but that didn't mean we were uncivilised. Well, not all of the time.

There was a moment of congestion when the truck with the sandbags arrived at the same time as an enormous delivery of food for the guests. Most of the food went into a freezer in Munty's kitchen and some in the fridge for our evening meal. We sent the builder's truck off to the first camp and wiped the bread around our eggy plates.

When we arrived at camp number one, Van Lloyd's men had checked out the tents and were installing a shower and a big barrel of water to feed the cistern and for general purposes — for the men to shave and for the ladies to wash their hair and do what other necessities had to be done before appearing in public.

The builder's truck arrived, and we unloaded half of the sandbags and sent the truck on to camp two with the other half. They were then to build the shooting positions that Stan had mapped out and come back to us to help out. Stan dished out the appropriate dollars to soothe their souls.

Surveying the scene, Stan didn't look happy.

'What's up, my friend?' I said.

'You realise what we have done,' Stan said, 'and it is entirely my fault, but the shooting positions are all built for an attack from the north. If they come at us from the west, we're not protected. The east is fine because it's sea, and the south is covered by the main camp. From the west, we're vulnerable. How could I be such an idiot?'

'Maybe we can hope that the poachers don't return today and they haven't thought of changing their plans. We can then get more sandbags to extend the shooting positions to the west. We'll have enough to build a beach by the end of this.'

'It sounds like lap-of-the-gods time,' he said. 'Oh, how I hate that.'

'In ancient times, when the Greeks wrote plays, they set up plot threads so complicated that they weren't able to tie the threads together and resolve. They just used to get the gods down from Olympus to do the ending. Maybe it's the same with us. The gods will be on our side.'

'We need some form of protection for the tourists,' he said. 'A smaller version of the stockade would do. Let's check out the second camp to see what still needs to be done.'

'Look on the bright side, Stan. We are professionals. They are raw recruits from local tribes and untrained in battle. They don't stand a chance. Whoever is in charge is likely to use them as cannon fodder. Doesn't seem right. Makes me struggle with my conscience.'

Stan, Bull and I got back in the jeep and Banti drove us for a brief inspection of the second camp — we could look in more detail later — and then on to the northern boundary to check on the fence. Would our defences there keep the poachers at bay?

We were about five minutes away from the fence when the walkie-talkie buzzed.

It was Red. 'We've got a problem. The poachers are back, and we've no defences built.'

'We're nearly with you,' I said. 'Keep them at bay until we arrive. Use the elephant gun on them if you have to. Fire on your bellies. Stay low. Shoot to cripple only if they shoot first, remember. If they start shooting to kill, then so will we.'

We told Banti to put his foot down. We could hear the sound of shooting and were hoist by our own petard. The jeep blocking the fence had provided the poachers with ideal cover. They could shoot at us from their newly protected position, and we were blocked off from returning fire. We had to move to the flanks to shoot at them from the sides.

I shouted at Banti to stop at what I thought was a safe distance. Stan, Bull and I jumped out of the jeep and hit the ground. Stan and I crawled on our bellies to the east, and Bull the west.

I surveyed the scene. The poachers must have thought the battle was all but won. Two of them were actually firing from the roof of our blocking jeep. Arrogant. A weakness. Stupid.

Red and Pieter provided covering fire while the three of us reinforcements crawled along the ground to our positions on the flanks. The firing from the poachers was coming not only from our jeep, forwards, but also from the roof of their jeep, behind. I counted five poachers. They were wasteful, scattering bullets all over the place seemingly at random with no targets in mind — they were kids having fun, and that gets you killed. We could wait for them to run out of ammunition, but that wouldn't achieve much — they'd just come back for more when re-equipped. Maybe they'd send their jeep off for ammo and the position would be unchanged.

I let off a round from the Uzi to see what they would do. Bull opened up from the left and there was swivelling from the second jeep to attack our flanks. That gave some relief to Red and Pieter from their positions in the centre.

I picked up the sniper rifle and looked through the telescopic sight. I lined up on one of the poachers on the top of our jeep. It would be a difficult shot — the sight was not set for this distance and the poacher was lying down, narrowing the target for me — but nothing ventured . . .

I fired and, as much by luck than judgement, caught the man in the hip. He dropped his assault rifle and reached down to touch the wound.

There was another exchange of fire between us, and it was stalemate. They weren't succeeding at their attack and we, pinned down, weren't whittling them down to any great degree. Then I had the idea. I spoke into the walkie-talkie. 'Red,' I said. 'Use the elephant gun and go for the fuel tank on our jeep.'

A massive boom came from the weapon and I could hear the sound of it hitting the metal of the chassis before plunging inside. The bullet struck its target and the fuel tank burst into flames.

The two men on that jeep stood no chance. The three on top of their backward jeep suffered the same fate as the fire spread and set their vehicle alight with another fireball.

Then the bullets from their Kalashnikovs exploded and we kept low and far away.

Pure mayhem.

I pressed the send button on the walkie-talkie. 'Everybody, give it a minute while we allow all ammunition to be spent before approaching. Careful. We don't know if there are others alive. Crawl, and let's meet up at a safe distance from the fire.'

There was no more firing at our positions as we advanced and stood up. There were five charred, unrecognisable bodies lying on top of the jeeps.

I looked around me. There wasn't a single animal in sight. Who says that animals aren't smart?

'Got any friends in the police department?' I asked Pieter. 'We're going to have to do a lot of sweet-talking to explain this. Be good to have a police officer on our side.'

* * *

The fire engine arrived first, putting out the flames and making everything safe. They carried the five victims from the top of the jeeps and laid them in a row while waiting for enough body bags. We gave the firemen a watered-down version of events, but I sensed they didn't believe it. In their place, I wouldn't have either.

A squad car followed around twenty minutes later and two police officers got out. One was young, tall and thin, and looked like he had Zulu heritage. The other was older, white, and had a beer-barrel chest that was just within the boundaries of his current uniform size.

'Good to see you, Pieter,' the older one said. 'Why do we meet in such surroundings? You guys been having fun, it looks like. Do I need to get out my notebook or will it all be a pack of lies?'

'Not a whole pack,' Pieter said.

The officer introduced himself to me as Captain Munroe. 'Who may you be?'

'Just a friend,' I said. 'Helping out an old mate. No one of consequence.'

'I see a lot of firearms here,' he said. 'Is that an Uzi? Don't see many of those around — Kalashnikovs are two a penny, but Uzis cost a packet. Brownings in the shoulder holsters. You guys been hunting squirrels?'

'Something like that,' I said. 'Had to reduce the population somehow.'

'Let's get this straight,' he said. 'I can't help you — and, boy, do you need help — if you don't tell me the truth. Go ahead, Pieter.'

'I called on you weeks ago,' Pieter said. 'Poachers? Ivory? Remember? You said you didn't have the resources to help guard the reserve.'

'So you decided it was a free-for-all and took the law into your own hands?'

'Have you ever seen an elephant die?' Pieter said. 'It's heartbreaking. These animals are majestic. Then they are taken for their tusks and die with their brains blown out and are fodder for the scavengers. Someone has to do something.'

'And you decided it had to be you?' Munroe said.

'Yes,' said Pieter. 'There was no other choice. We got here today and the poachers were lined up before we even arrived. Shooting like crazy. No one in the firing line was safe. We stopped them. End of.'

'How many more of you?' he said.

'Three,' said Pieter.

'All with experience, I take it, by looking at your weapons?' Munroe said.

'We're a good team,' I said, 'otherwise it would be us lined up on the ground.'

'Is this the end?' Munroe said.

'That's up to the poachers.'

'Pieter,' he said, 'you do make life difficult. By rights, I should take you in and give you the third degree, but your heart's in the right place. I don't have the officers or budget to station anyone here. They'd be scared out of their wits, too, at the prospect of a lion watching them with slavering mouth. What can I do to help you, within my power?'

'Use a police officer's sight,' I said, 'and turn a blind eye.'

* * *

We regrouped at the second camp, where preparations were going well. All the tents were checked and were fit for the guests, a large fire had been built with cushions surrounding it and a barbecue ready for the evening meals, and best of all, Van Lloyd's men were rigging up electric fences, powered by portable energisers, around the perimeter. They should keep hungry animals at bay. It had been a good morning and we were still alive. OK, so the enemy had been inexperienced kids, but maybe today would deter others to sign up. I'd settle for that.

Pieter gave instructions that when the men had finished here, they should go to the north fence and repair the section of electrified fencing there. The jeeps could stay there as a barricade and as a reminder to the poachers of what they could expect from us. We'd been lucky not to have lost any animals when that section was down.

The five of us sat around the unlit fire and we all wished we had brought some cold beers. Then our wish was granted. Ranu arrived with exactly that, telling us it had been Ibo's idea. Ibo went up further in my esteem. We sipped and were silent for a while.

'Good shooting, Red,' I said.

'Could hardly miss,' he replied, 'but still satisfying. I feel sorry for the men who died. It wasn't their war, not what they signed up for. Shoot an elephant, saw off its tusks and be off. There'll be a few wives and children shedding tears tonight.'

'I wonder what the poachers will do next,' said Stan. 'Be good to have a new plan ready.'

'They'll not stop,' said Bull. 'They've invested too much here. They could just move on to another reserve, but they will be smarting after today. Their pride has been hurt, and they'll want to get that back. Maybe the elephants are a secondary target now. The first is us. Not good for their reputation if they are seen to be defeated. They won't stop until we are gone. Dead or alive. Dead is what I reckon.'

I rolled the beer bottle over my forehead and then took a big mouthful. Nectar.

'There's elephants in the reserve, but also one in this room, metaphorically speaking,' I said.

Bull looked at me and nodded.

'Bull knows,' I said. 'Reveal all.'

'The poachers knew we were coming,' said Bull.

'Exactly,' I said. 'We've got ourselves a spy.'

CHAPTER SEVEN

'Pieter,' the woman said, when we arrived back at base, 'where have you been? You've been neglecting me. You're a naughty boy.'

The woman was shorter than average, with long blonde hair — not natural, I would guess by her eyebrows — showing under her straw hat. Sixty years old was my guess, judging by the layers of make-up worn to blend in with the facelift. She was wearing a sand-coloured outfit of short-sleeved blouse and starched shorts like she was playing the heroine in *The Mummy*. I had a sneaky feeling that she would be scary, too.

'Pieter, who are these people? You must introduce me.'

'Folks, this is Penelope.'

'Never Penny,' she butted in.

'And here is Johnny, Stan, Red and Bull,' said Pieter. 'They're here as part of a government military exercise.'

'How tedious for you,' she said. 'Hence all the guns. Frightening.'

'Mostly blanks,' I said.

'Still,' she said, 'I think you won't get under our feet.'

'Quiet as a church mouse,' said Bull.

'Well, you just get on with what you need to do, and Pieter and I will keep out of your way.'

'Why did you come here?' said Pieter. 'I thought you'd left for England.'

'I had so much fun I thought I'd extend my holiday. I did text you, or at least I think I did, although the phone has a habit of doing what it wants to do rather than what you want it to do. Refreshments. I'm gasping. I'd like a martini like Munty makes, Pieter. Have you tried her cooking, boys? To die for. So authentic.'

'A gem,' I said. 'Could have been here all her life.'

'Now you're teasing,' she said. 'Johnny, was it? While we're waiting for the drink, Pieter, you can take my suitcase to our tent.'

'But there is no tent,' Pieter said. 'We're fully booked. Everyone arrives tomorrow. All the tents are allocated. I'm sharing the big tent with these guys.'

'I don't suppose they will mind being turfed out for a few days — more like a week, I suppose. They can make do somewhere.'

'But there isn't an elsewhere,' Pieter protested.

'Think laterally, darling Pieter.' She waved her hand dismissively. 'There is the first camp. They can move there, where they won't be a nuisance. Good. That's settled. Where is that drink? Boy,' she called to Ibo, 'chase that drink.'

'But, ma'am,' said Bull, creating a diversion while the drink was being made and buying Ibo some time, 'part of the training exercise is that we stay to protect you all the time.'

'Trivia.' She waved her hand again. If she did that once more, I might explode. 'Let's compromise. You can stay until after dinner.'

Where was the compromise in that? We were already going to do that.

'You must remember I will have Pieter to protect me,' she said, simpering.

I looked at Bull and he shrugged. The others did the same. We were better off getting out of here. I dare say all of us felt sorry for Pieter — those that live by the sword, as some might cruelly say. We would mount guard whatever her instructions. I had a feeling Pieter was going to be occupied most of the time.

We dismantled our table for five back down to four and sat ourselves down. Ibo, unbidden, brought us four beers and a plate of beef sandwiches.

'So, we have someone working for the opposition,' I said. 'One of our rangers is playing a double game. I have a plan to smoke him out.'

'One of your famous plans,' said Red. 'Does this involve us getting shot at, by any chance?'

'Not entirely.'

'Which means yes,' said Bull. 'Go on. Hit us with it.'

'What would you do if you were the poachers and knew our movements tomorrow?'

'Why not today?' Stan said.

'The poachers will be licking their wounds,' I said. 'They'll need to recruit some replacements, too. Tomorrow will be the earliest they can mount another attack.' I held back from waving dismissively myself. Seemed like it was catching. 'Returning to my original question, what would you do in their place? There are two alternatives. Avoid us, or take us on?'

'They are here for ivory,' said Stan. 'They have made an investment here. They won't go before they fill their boots. They can't afford to quit yet. We are their problem. They'll take us on. Take us out of the equation. Revert to situation normal.'

'Their pride will have been dented, too,' said Bull. 'They'll strike out rather than try to wait us out.'

'They won't wait long,' Red put in. 'Every day that passes, they'll be losing opportunities to make money. Tomorrow is my bet for reaction.'

'They will know our numbers,' I said. 'The informant will have told them that. They'll be encouraged by the fact that there are only five of us. They'll underestimate our strengths. Anyone would. You don't come up against teams like us more than once in a lifetime. Were we superior to them, they'll ask themselves, or was today's skirmish just pure luck? If the poachers know in advance where we will be tomorrow morning, then they'll think they have the element of surprise.'

'So tell us the plan,' said Stan.

I did.

The reaction was as I had hoped. There were risks involved in splitting our forces, and it was a dangerous gamble, but everyone was up for it. Faint heart and all that

We finished our beers and sandwiches and loudly declared we were off to check on the west of the reserve. There was an argument about who would drive. We played rock, paper, scissors to decide and, thankfully, Red lost. Stan won and jumped in the driver's seat. We were off for another adventure.

For the route to the west we took a fork in the road in between the two camps. As we drove, we were hoping to see some new animals, with the west providing cover among the trees and the lush ground leading up the mountains. We were also nervous, in case we got on the wrong side of the elephants. When we got to a good spot for assessing the fences, Stan turned the jeep around ready for a quick exit.

We sat there and saw our first zebra. So graceful, such wonderful camouflage. I thought it might outrun the lions and leopards, if spotted. Its chances would be less good, though, if lionesses acted in a pack of three or more, as they were accustomed to do.

'Any thoughts, gentlemen?' I said.

'Wrong terrain for us,' said Stan. 'The foothills of the mountain would be the best place to attack and that's on their side of the fence. Too much cover for them and nothing for us. We can't rely on the jeep to act as a defence — they saw what happened to jeeps this morning.'

'What are our chances of taking the mountains first?' said Bull. 'Pick them off from the hills?'

'It would mean splitting our forces,' said Stan. 'Not a good thing. Johnny, what do you reckon on the sniper rifle?'

'I could try. I could do a couple of tests while we're here and make adjustments to the sight to give myself a fair chance of shooting anyone who ventures close enough to me.'

'Will you need backup?' said Red, 'or is this a one-man attack?'

'Johnny acts to weaken their flank and we fire belly down from here,' said Stan. 'We might be able to provide some cover with any loose branches from the tree, but I guess bullets would just penetrate and go on to us. I don't like it. Once Johnny exposes his position, the focus will be on him. I reckon one of us should go, too.'

'I volunteer,' said Bull. 'It seems my *raison d'être* in life is to dig Johnny Silver out of a hole and I don't see why that should change now. We can't let him loose on his own — we never know what mischief he'll get up to.'

'What are we going to do with Pieter?' said Stan. 'Can we count on him as a part of the plan? Is he in or is he out?'

'I can't see him getting away from Penelope's clutches,' I said. 'Best to leave him as some sort of defence of the base camp. Someone has to welcome the new guests tomorrow so, all told, he probably has enough on his plate.'

'If you don't mind me saying so,' said Stan, 'it is all looking a bit thin. We will be down to two sets of two, rather than one unit of five. It's a pretty weak set-up.'

'We've been in worse,' Red said. 'I'll do a Comanche rain dance tonight and pray to Manitou to obscure their vision.'

'Can't do any harm,' said Bull, 'although I've never seen it work before.'

'Have faith,' said Red. 'Maybe this time it will. Be an entertainment for Penelope, too. Might keep her off our backs for a while.'

'I'm willing to try anything,' I said. 'As long as you don't want me to join in.'

While everyone was scoping out the fence and making sure the current was still on, I went back to the jeep, fetched the sniper rifle and lay down on the grass. If the enemy was drawn to where we would leave the jeep, it would be a decent distance from the mountains. I estimated that as around six hundred feet — well within the effective range of the monster sniper rifle, which was one thousand feet. I looked through the telescopic sight and sought out a rock of about the same distance.

The first bullet went high, so I turned the adjustment screw down.

I fired another and it was close — just little too much to right. I changed the setting to the left and fired off one more bullet.

Perfect. The plan might just work.

'Elephants!' shouted Stan.

I raced back to the jeep and jumped in. The others were already seated. As Stan fired up the engine and we began to make progress, I saw the elephants. Around twelve of them, in a group of adults and children. All the adults had the prized tusks that the poachers sought. One adult started a run towards us — Pieter told us that elephants have a matriarchal society, so this elephant was most probably a female, leader of the group and protector of the young. We had invaded their land, and that was an affront to them. We must be taught a lesson. That was not a good sign.

We sped away and I looked back. The female elephant had upped her pace. You wouldn't think an elephant could reach such a speed. Then she stopped. Not worth chasing. She had made her point.

'This rather complicates matters,' said Stan. 'Red and I would be extremely vulnerable. While firing, we would have to keep a lookout for elephants and be ready to drive away instantly. I'm not sure how much use we would be to you two.'

'We'll have the high ground,' I said. 'Good defensive position if we start to be attacked. They expose themselves while they climb up. We just have to accept that we will be out-numbered. If the worst comes to the worst, you could exit the reserve, drive up the mountain and try to support us — it's a long drive, though. I'm not sure if Bull and I could hold out that long. Maybe all the shooting will keep the elephants away.'

'It sounds like there are a lot of maybes,' said Red.

'It was ever thus,' I said.

'Doesn't make it any the better,' said Bull. 'We just have to accept the situation and roll with it.'

'Any thoughts on tonight?' I said to Stan. 'The problem of the dreaded Penelope?'

'I don't think we can rely on Pieter for guard duty,' he said. 'There would be one of the rangers as security, but that ranger won't have the same resources and experience as us. We have to supplement him. Bearing in mind that one of the rangers is working for the opposition and we don't know which one, we need to keep watch throughout the night. Two-hour shifts should do it. Any preferences?'

'I'll take any slot when Penelope should be asleep,' said Bull. 'The way she treats Ibo winds me up. I suspect I'm on the cusp of losing my rag and tipping a martini over her head tonight at dinner, or anything more shocking that I can come up with.'

'I'll take the first slot, then,' I said. 'Stan next, then Bull and finally Red at dawn, when the light will work best with his eyesight. No offence.'

'None taken,' he said.

'Bull and I will depart an hour before dawn for the mountains,' I said, 'and Stan and Red should start a half hour after us for the place we checked out. Sun Tzu said that when starting a war you should know your enemy and know yourself. Strengths and weaknesses on both counts. Well, guys, we can't put it off any longer. Back to base camp for dinner and to do some packing. Once more into the breach.'

* * *

When we arrived back, it was time for the plan to be executed. I commandeered the office and called Banti inside. There was something about him that didn't ring true with me — was it simply that he was not tall and thin like the other rangers, too well fed? Whatever, he was my prime candidate for the mole.

'We've drawn up our plans for tomorrow,' I said. 'You will be with us at the west fence checking it and the electrics. We'll meet you there half an hour after dawn. Anything we need to know?'

'Elephant country,' he said. 'Dangerous place. Bring lots of darts for the dart gun and bullets for the elephant gun, too. Don't stay long. We usually drive the bus through without stopping.'

'See you in the morning,' I said.

The next up was Ranu. Same speech with one change. We were supposed to meet him at the east fence one hour after dawn, check the boundaries on the side running down to the sea was the excuse.

And so it went. Ackta was the north side, where we had tackled the poachers, one and a half hours after dawn. Lastly Smarfy, the side running down from the base camp to the southernmost tip of the reserve, two hours after dawn.

The trap was set. Who would take the bait? If it worked, of course.

We sat down at our normal place while, quite separate and distanced, there was another table laid with cutlery, serviette, salt and pepper, and proper wine glasses rather than tumblers. Didn't take long to work out who that was for, seeing as the guests hadn't arrived yet.

Ibo looked across at Bull and smiled. Bull nodded. Two minutes later, the cold beers arrived. We sipped and sighed. I could smell the barbecue searing a piece of meat and tried hard not to salivate.

Pieter appeared. He was in dark-blue chinos with a light-blue short-sleeved shirt and a black tie. I hoped the tie wasn't an omen.

'What are you wearing?' I said.

'Penelope likes to dress for dinner. This is as formal as I could get.'

Bull smiled and shook his head as he tried not to belly-laugh.

'She's got you dead under her thumb, hasn't she?' Bull said. 'Do I hear wedding bells?'

'Will need a divorce first,' Pieter said. 'I'm keeping my fingers crossed. She's unstoppable. Won't stop talking — make that won't stop giving orders. She said she wanted springbok tonight and Munty had to get it out of the freezer when she had impala marinating. Munty is not happy. The way Penelope treats Ibo is not helping either. I despair. Since you're part of the army, I shouldn't mingle with you — commissioned officers only are worthy of being talked to.'

'Maybe she will change when the other guests arrive,' I said.

'Do you honestly believe that?' Pieter said.

'No,' I said. 'I was just trying to cheer you up. "Situation dire" is more apt.'

'So, what's up with you guys?' Pieter said.

'We've set a trap for the informer,' Stan said. 'Whatever you do, don't let the rangers talk to one another. Tomorrow morning we will fight the Chinese again, if the bait is taken. Tell us about elephants.'

'Why elephants?' Pieter said.

'Because we are going to fight in their territory,' said Stan. 'What will they do? Watch us, or trample over us with those terrible feet?'

'How long is this skirmish going to last?' Pieter said.

'As you know,' said Stan, 'battles don't last long. I estimate fifteen minutes only. It will either work, and work quickly, or we will be running for home. So, elephants?'

'Your only hope is that they will be at the southern section of the west fence,' Pieter said. 'It will take them about that time to get to you.'

'How do they react to shooting?' said Red. 'Will the noise keep them away? Do say yes.'

'They will come and investigate,' Pieter said. 'Then it's up to them — they might just retreat, watch or charge.'

'Comanches have a way with animals,' Red said. 'They can talk to the animals and commune with them. The whisper, it is called. Can you commune with elephants?'

'After a while they get used to you and largely ignore you,' Pieter said. 'You can't teach them to follow orders, but you can hope to be part of their group.'

'And how do you do that?' said Red.

'It takes about three months to condition them and not to see you as a threat. You can't do anything in a day. The best I can do to help is to say keep the engine running on the jeep. You do not stand a chance against elephants.'

'Well,' Bull said, 'we've all been reassured by this little chat. We'll all sleep soundly in our beds tonight. Thanks for that, Pieter.'

'Don't shoot the messenger. You asked a question and I answered it.'

'Boys, boys,' I said, 'play nicely. Because of the charming Penelope, we're effectively a man down — you, that is. We need to make changes in our method of combatting the Chinese. You have one job tomorrow, Pieter — watch the south entrance to this camp. Call us if you are under attack here. We'll respond as quickly as we can. Practise tomorrow morning and keep it up when the guests arrive. When is that?'

'Mid-afternoon, if the planes are on time. We're down to sixteen after four cancellations. Van Lloyd isn't a happy bunny. A clause in the booking allowed people to cancel up to twenty-four hours before departure — the four squeaked in.'

'What a shame,' I said. 'My heart bleeds. Back to important matters. Don't let Penelope divert you. One job, Pieter, just one job. Don't let us down.'

There was the sound of a false cough from Pieter's tent. Penelope was standing outside unmoving in a long white dress with blue piping around the edges and a pair of gold sandals. Her hair was scraped back and held by two tortoiseshell combs, revealing a large pair of gold hooped earrings dangling down. She had forgotten her tiara.

'Pieter,' she said, 'time to escort me to dinner.' She held out her arm.

He walked over to her, took her arm and then the pair walked slowly, unmissably, to the table that was set.

If Penelope had any empathy she would have detected the listless signs of a man just obeying orders. If we had been nearer to him, we would have, no doubt, heard him sigh.

Penelope waved and caught Ibo's eye. He listened to the first of what I suspected would be many orders and scurried off. A jug of water and a martini arrived, with a cold beer for Pieter. Penelope frowned at the beer — not enough class, I presume — but you have to cut someone a little slack every once in a while.

'I think we can have one drink tonight from the vodka store, Stan,' I said. 'Do the honours, and we'll show her what class really is, and what Pieter would enjoy if he had an unfettered choice available to him. One act of defiance. Petty, but there you go.'

Ibo emerged from Munty's kitchen carrying two plates of — never any doubt — springbok, and set them before Penelope and Pieter. She said something to him and he came back with a bottle of wine: red was all I could tell. We sipped our vodka like connoisseurs, which we were, as long as vodka was involved.

Ibo came over and asked us if we wanted him to serve us dinner. We told him he had enough on his plate, before realising the pun. We asked him for four more beers. The small glass of vodka downed, we went to the barbecue. Our springbok steaks were resting — they looked familiar.

'Looks good, Munty,' I said.

She leaned closer to us. 'Impala,' she whispered. 'The lady will never taste the difference.'

One point to Team Safari.

Munty put an impala steak on our plates and we helped ourselves to a side of potatoes in butter with some green herbs.

Back at our table, Ibo handed us the beers.

'We need your help again tomorrow, Ibo,' I said. 'Man the base station like last time, except there will be, I guess, no Pieter on duty. We want you to take up post at dawn. We're sorry about the early start, but there will be a lot of action in the morning.'

'Honoured,' he said. 'Will it be exciting?'

'More than exciting,' Bull said. 'If there was a word for more than exciting, I would use it. Hurry along, my friend. The lady appears to have finished and will get demanding again. Don't forget to bow like the slave she thinks you are. One day she will pay for it. Never fear.'

The impala was excellent and was deemed so with enthusiasm by Penelope. She got up from the table a little unsteadily and weaved her way slowly to the facilities. The gait was more prominent on the slower way back, and she sat down and summoned Ibo.

There were raised voices. I could easily hear her shout when Ibo told her that they didn't have any decaffeinated coffee.

Bull made a move to get up.

'Hold.' I placed my hand on his arm. 'There'll be a time when we take her down, but it is not this time. We've got too much to do to have a further complication. I have a feeling she'll be snoring soon, and in the morning we'll shout at her when she has a sore head. Small victory, but a victory nonetheless.'

Pieter looked at us and shrugged helplessly. 'I have no control of her', the gesture seemed to say. How can such a strong man be so weak? In the past, he had taken on enemies in Africa and Europe and killed men when there was no option. Now he was a passenger, and, where nothing was possible, he had succumbed to a dominating woman who deserved whatever we would mete out to her.

Bide your time, Johnny. Bide your time. The gods will come down and finish the play.

'Time for the watch to start,' I said. 'You guys get back to the first camp and send Bull to replace me. If someone gets to replace Bull, we'll both get a couple of hours sleep before the deadline of pre-dawn.'

We resisted the lure of the boiled milk dessert, which would be, no doubt, reincarnated for breakfast. Not that we would need one. A cold beer would be nice if the outcomes of the morning plans were favourable.

We got up from the table. I caught Ibo's eye, silently saying he had done well, and to be awake by dawn. I complimented Munty on the food, picked up a chair and dragged it close to the fire. After putting three logs on I sat with my Uzi across my lap, the Browning in its holster and monster sniper at my side. If there was to be any action, bring it on.

CHAPTER EIGHT

Bull and I set off for the mountains, first on a road, then a track and then just anywhere we could navigate with the 4x4. It was made even more tricky by the fact we turned off the lights just in case anyone was watching. Hairy.

We parked the jeep as best we could and were satisfied no one would spot its blackness against the dark of the mountain. We scrambled up to the rocks we had spotted the day before. As the sun rose, a startling red sky spread widely across the horizon. I checked in with Ibo. Nothing to report. On the other side of the fence, I could see a jeep, with Stan driving. Wise man. Now it was just a case of waiting with crossed fingers, hoping that the plan had worked.

It didn't take long. I heard the sound of the engines in the silence of the night and saw four pinpricks from the headlights of two vehicles.

Banti, you've been a naughty boy.

I called up Red and told him to keep the channel open continuously so I could hear their progress. Then it was time for the fun to begin.

The vehicles parked well away from the area where the fighting would begin. They'd learned their lesson. Ten men climbed out of the vehicles — one jeep and one truck — and walked to a point they must have deemed to be a safe distance away from where Stan and Red's jeep was parked.

They had been too cautious. They couldn't fire effectively on us from that distance, and we were out of their range. Something had to give.

We were in no hurry. I could hit targets with the sniper rifle and pick them off one by one.

'Start moving forward, belly down,' I said to Red. 'Fire off to see what their response is.'

The poachers must have estimated the odds were on their side — ten of them and, seemingly, just two of us — and began to move forward. Stan let off a round of bullets and the poachers stopped to assess the situation, then moved forward again.

'I'll fire the first shot in one minute,' I said. 'They'll be puzzled and fearful. Move forward then.'

I lined up on the man that seemed to be giving orders, held my breath so that there was no involuntary movement of the rifle, and fired.

The man went down clutching his back — my adjustments to the sights had been worthwhile. I fired again and shot another man in his head.

The poachers were disoriented, looking in all directions for where the shots were coming from. That cleared the way for Stan and Red. They fired two bursts from the Kalashnikovs, and three men fell to the ground. The odds were then only five against, it would seem, to three of us.

'Moving forward,' said Stan.

'Moving forward,' said Bull. 'Ducks in a gallery. Bam, bam.'

I continued to pick off targets, reckoning that some of the men were hit by more than one of us. No such thing as overkill in a battle.

I put down the sniper rifle and climbed down from the safety of the mountains, then prepared to fire the Uzi. I shot a volley in the side of the group and caught two more.

Soon it was all over. There were no poachers left.

Except one. He stood up and raised his rifle.

'Lay down your arms or prepare to die,' I said.

While he was working out what to do, I laid the Uzi on the ground and took out my Browning from its shoulder holster.

'Lay down your arms or prepare to die,' I repeated.

He swung up the Kalashnikov in my direction.

I put a bullet between his eyes. He had chosen the wrong alternative. Senseless.

'Ibo,' I said into the walkie-talkie. 'Contact Captain Munroe and tell him to come to the west fence on the opposite of our side. He won't be able to miss it. Tell him to bring an ambulance, too. Maybe two.'

I picked up the sniper rifle and Uzi, and Bull and I climbed down the whole way from the mountain and stood surveying the scene. Carnage. Bodies all over the place, some just injured. I made the body count seven. I hoped Munroe would get information from the survivors.

Stan came through. He sounded agitated. 'We have a problem. Elephants are between us and the jeep. The motor's running, but we can't get to it.'

I looked across at them. Stan and Red were cut off. We could try shooting at the elephants, but I guessed it would be futile, if not downright dangerous — we would have to shoot through Stan and Red to get to them. There was a risk, too, of any more shooting spooking them and bringing about a stampede.

Stan and Red just stood there, only delaying the inevitable. Then Red moved forward in a straight line to the lead elephant — the matriarch, it would be. He had his hands in the air and the index and little fingers pointing up and the middle fingers closed like he had done yesterday. I could hear some sort of chanting coming from the walkie-talkie.

The elephant just stood there looking at Red, trying to work out what was going on. Was this strange man friend or foe? Was he just plain mad?

Red stepped a pace forward, and the elephant did the same. They were within touching distance.

The elephant uncurled her trunk and smelled Red up and down.

Red patted her trunk.

The elephant turned round and led the herd back to where they had come.

We were all transfixed. We couldn't believe what we had witnessed.

Red took a bow. 'An old Comanche ritual when stranded in front of a buffalo. Didn't know if it would work, but there was no other option. Worth a beer?'

'No,' I said. 'Worth a crate of beer. You guys get back to base camp and wallow in what has happened this morning. We'll stay here for Munroe and lay it all before him. If we don't see you for lunch, you may have to think of a way of breaking us out of jail. Maybe there's a Comanche ritual for that.'

I spoke to Ibo and told him he could stand down.

'What was that I heard?' he said. 'Did Red communicate with a matriarch?'

'You wouldn't believe it, even if you saw it through your own eyes,' I said. 'What's Pieter doing at the moment?'

'He is looking after the Penelope lady. She says she is feeling bad this morning. I have had to get the first-aid kit.'

'I told you we could get some revenge, and at least Pieter's dignity is preserved.'

'I don't know what that means,' said Ibo.

'Come to think of it,' I said, 'I don't either.'

Bull and I sat on their jeep, which, of course, I immediately commandeered to replenish our stocks, and looked at each other.

'Do you believe what we have just witnessed?' I said.

'No more so than you.' He shook his head. 'Maybe there's something higher in life that we don't understand.'

'Maybe,' I said. 'It's too early in the day for me to discuss philosophy or spirituality matters. Especially when all the time my mind is focused on a cold beer. Maybe it's better for around the campfire.'

'Maybe.'

'Maybe we could see which one of us could speak the shortest sentence?' I said.

'Yep.'

'You win.'

Munroe's Land Rover pulled up beside us. He got out and took in the scene. 'How did we get such carnage? Stray shots from a squirrel cull? Some unfortunate people caught in a crossfire?'

'I can see why you've progressed up the ladder so fast,' I said. 'You must be psychic.'

'OK, guys,' he said, 'what really happened?'

'We set a trap for the poachers,' I said.

'And they walked right in,' said Bull.

An ambulance pulled up beside us. The crew was as incredulous as Munroe. They radioed for reinforcements.

'They underestimated us,' I said.

'Easy to do,' Munroe said. 'No offence.'

'None taken,' said Bull. 'Or perhaps just a little bit.'

'We suckered them in here,' I said. 'They must have thought they would have the advantage of surprise, when in fact we were here waiting for them.'

'So did you give them the chance to surrender?'

'Not as such,' I said.

'Exactly,' said Bull.

'So the answer to that is no?'

'They had the opportunity to surrender when I fired the first bullet,' I said. 'I hit a man in the back rather than to kill. They knew they outnumbered us and made the wrong decision.'

Munroe looked at our weapons leaning on the side of the Land Rover. 'Is that a monster sniper rifle I see?'

'Very good,' I said. 'You know your weapons.'

'Packs a punch,' he said. 'Pinpoint accuracy. Lethal in the right hands.'

'Which are mine,' I said.

'Modesty not your strong suit?'

'I haven't seemed to have been punished for it.'

'Me, neither,' said Bull. 'Whatever that means.'

'Recap,' said Munroe. 'Ten poachers — now dead or injured — arrive to teach you a lesson. You're waiting for them, the two of you?'

'Four,' I said. 'Red and Stan are on the other side of the fence.'

'I stand corrected,' Munroe said. 'Ten bad guys and four of you. You, Silver, fire the first shot and all hell breaks loose. All the opposition reduced to bodies on the ground. Am I right so far?'

'Sounds good to me,' said Bull. 'Improves in the telling.'

'You do make life difficult,' said Munroe. 'What am I supposed to do with you?'

'I think,' I said, 'that you could let us go. Technically, I fired first, but if you are confronted by ten men carrying Kalashnikovs, what are you supposed to do? Look on the bright side: you now have three prisoners to sweat. They might lead you to the top man, everything tickety-boo.'

'I fail to see that seven dead can be tickety-boo,' he said. 'What do you propose to do now? What have you achieved?'

'Hopefully, I would like them to see they are outclassed and move on,' I said. 'I imagine you would like the same. Back to the easy job of sitting comfortably in your office chair.'

'Do you know what ivory is worth?' Munroe said. 'The market for ivory is worth twenty-three billion dollars. Twenty-three billion! An average pair of tusks can sell for a hundred thousand dollars. If you want to steal some, there is a lot at stake. Who is going to stand in your way? Not a bunch of outdated mercenaries. They'll keep coming at you until you have no option but to run. They'll wear you down, picking you off one by one. Shooting to kill. Be sensible. Pack your bags and quit.'

'We came to help an old friend,' I said. 'We'll stick around until he doesn't need help anymore. To leave now would be without honour.'

'And honour is one of the things that drives us,' said Bull. 'You can't turn your back on a friend. That's what friendship is all about. We don't quit.'

Munroe sighed. 'Why me? What did I do to deserve this? Go on, the pair of you. Get out of here before I change my mind and get heavy-handed.'

Bull and I picked up our weapons and started the long climb to where we had hidden our jeep.

'Turned out nice again,' said Bull.

* * *

We arrived back at base camp in time for sandwiches and cold beers with Red and Stan. Red had the widest of smiles on his face. Stan just looked stunned.

There was about three hours to go before the guests arrived. We would use that time effectively. I called Pieter over from his table with Penelope, who was looking rather frail. My heart bled for her. She obviously didn't know that the best cure for a hangover was a bacon sandwich with Worcester sauce. Never fails for me, although, obviously, I don't tend to drink enough to get a hangover. God forbid.

'You've heard the full story from Red and Stan here, I presume,' I said, 'but there's work still to do.'

'Strange incident with the elephant, Red,' he said. 'I've never heard anything like that before. Phew! How lucky can one man be?'

'More things in heaven and earth and all that, as the saying goes,' Bull said.

'How is Penelope, and what's your availability?' I said.

'Bad on both counts. She has a hangover and I'm playing nursemaid. I have a welcome speech to work through for the guests. I'd like to help, but can't seem to fit it in.'

'I hate to say this,' said Bull, 'but I'm detecting a tee-ny-weeny bit of a lack of commitment from you. We came all this way to help you and you're absent most of the time. You need to get your priorities in order, Pieter.'

'At the moment,' I said, 'we need to find Banti. He didn't show up this morning on the west fence, and I can't see him here. He's been working with the poachers, feeding them information. We need to get the full picture of what he's told them. For that, we might need an interpreter. We need to pay him a visit. That's where you come in, Pieter. You are going to tell Penelope to lie down, then you are going to rehearse your welcome speech in the jeep. We leave in thirty minutes.'

'But—'

'No buts, Pieter,' I said. 'Get yourself together. We're going on a trip, like it or not.'

As Pieter left our table, Bull shook his head. 'If he doesn't shape up, the four of us are going to have to talk about whether we quit. There would be no dishonour in that.'

Red and Stan nodded.

'Agreed, reluctantly,' I said. 'You can't help a man who won't help himself.'

'What did you make of Munroe's speech about the worth of ivory and its implications?' Bull said.

'More than I ever had in mind about how much of the pair of tusks would sell for,' I said. 'You realise the position?'

'We're going to have to take them out,' Bull said. 'They're not going to leave of their own accord.'

'I'll need to take a detailed look at the place they're operating from,' said Stan. 'With planning, it's never too soon to start.'

'I'll do a dance to Manitou for our safety,' Red said. 'After the incident with the elephant this morning, do any of you believe that it won't work?'

Silence.

'I'd like to have a shower now, but there's no time,' said Stan. 'I'll try to fit that in before the guests arrive. Wash the smell of death from me. It always lingers.'

'What was it you told us earlier, Johnny?' Bull said. 'The key to war is know your enemy and know yourselves. Good book,' he added. 'Would have been better with pictures.'

'I didn't know you'd read it,' I said.

'Man's got to do something during those long hours on guard,' he said.

'As to the enemy,' I said, 'we know the Chinese are controlling the operation and have a seemingly limitless budget.'

'And they can recruit men whenever they need them,' said Stan. 'Cannon fodder mainly, but enough to make a difference. Won't be long until they get lucky and can overwhelm us.'

'As to knowing ourselves, we are a man down until Pieter wakes up to the enormity of the task we face,' I said. 'Could be crucial. I don't like it. We've never fought when we haven't been all together. An adjustment will need to be made. Our fighting capacity is down twenty per cent. I don't like it, I'll say it again. I don't see it as a good omen.'

'Unlike you to be pessimistic,' said Stan. 'No reason to feel unhappy after such a successful morning.'

'Apologies, guys. As you say, it's not like me. Maybe I'm just reacting to the fight — senseless lives lost — and what we know must be coming,' I said. 'But another plus point from this morning is that we seem to have Munroe on our side. Smiles all round. Break open another bottle of vodka tonight for a one-drink restorative.'

'Sounds like common sense,' said Bull. 'Nothing can look bleak after a vodka. Same guard duty tonight?'

'Two camps to watch over,' I said. 'Here, with sixteen guests coming, and ours, where we hope to get some peace. Not a great opportunity for sleep. We've had worse in the past, though.'

'The downside of having a free evening,' said Bull, 'is that we have to endure Penelope again. I've been wondering . . . Do you think Munty slipped something into Penelope's food?'

'If so,' I said, 'she will go up even higher in my esteem.'

'Be interesting to see how Ibo interacts with the guests,' said Bull. 'Hopefully they won't be as dismissive as Penelope. That they won't treat him just like a slave, with all the value judgements that go with it. I've got an idea about him, but I need to talk it over with Pieter, who seems to have little time for anything other than being Penelope's personal servant.'

'Talking of Pieter,' I said, 'let's round him up and track down Banti. OK, Bull, my friend, let's go and drag him away from his other duties.'

'I'll scope out the Chinese location while Red keeps watch here,' said Stan.

Bull and I drained our beers and got up from the table. We walked to the big tent, capable of holding five people, although not comfortably, which was currently occupied by Penelope and Pieter. He was standing with his back to us and looking down at the unfortunate occupant of the bed. He registered our presence — thankfully something of a promise that he could still function as a mercenary.

'I won't be long,' he said to Penelope. 'There's a bottle of water at your left hand. Drink lots and join me when the guests arrive. We could try the hair of the dog, but maybe that's too radical right now. Let's see.'

We left the tent and got into one of the jeeps. Bull drove while I took Pieter through what he needed to cover in his welcome speech for the guests. It wasn't difficult — he'd probably used it many times, with the only new element being the story relating to our presence and a hell of a lot of guns.

Banti lived in a village within a village. On a larger scale, it might have been called a township. Back from the main hub of the village, it looked like it would be classified as an 'informal settlement' or 'squatter camp'. The buildings were little more than shacks made of miscellaneous materials purloined from disused dwellings — concrete slabs as walls and corrugated iron for the roofs. In a country with so much wealth, how could so many people suffer so much poverty?

We approached and came across a woman dressed in a long black dress, sitting outside a shack, peeling vegetables. Pieter asked her what place was Banti's.

She shook her head.

Pieter asked again, but louder this time. From a shack about thirty yards away, a figure emerged and started to run.

'Take him down,' I shouted at Bull.

Bull deftly lifted the Browning from its holster and fired off a bullet. The man, obviously Banti, stumbled, but continued to run. Bull fired again and Banti fell to the ground.

'Shouldn't have needed the second bullet,' he said.

'Moving target, close to the effective range of the gun, wind blowing left to right,' I said. 'Don't beat yourself up about it.'

Pieter went to Banti, dragged him upright and manhandled him to the hut from which he had escaped. We sat him down in a rickety chair and looked about us. There were blankets covering the door and at two places inside to give the occupants some semblance of privacy. Candles were positioned in three places to create some light. There were two further chairs and a table. Placed on a table at the back of the hut was an impala, half skinned.

'He's been poaching my animals,' Pieter said. 'What a cheek! I give him a job and pay him fair wages and this is how he treats me. Killing the animals that he is supposed to be protecting. He deserves whatever the police do with him.'

'That can wait,' I said. 'Our priority is the poachers who kill the elephants. We need a complete picture. Let's get the story.'

Bull stood threateningly close to Banti and examined his leg. 'No exit wounds. He's going to have to go to hospital to get the bullets removed.'

'We'll call an ambulance, and Munroe, when we've finished with him,' I said. 'First, the facts. How did it start, Banti?'

'A man was waiting for me as I was coming home,' he said. 'He gave me some money and said they wanted information

— just where I and the other rangers would be the next day. They also said to ignore any breaks in the fence. It didn't seem to hurt, so I said I would do as he asked. He gave me money each week.'

'Didn't it occur to you that he was after ivory and would kill an elephant for it?'

'The man said he'd only kill a couple of elephants,' Banti said. 'We had plenty, so I agreed.'

Pieter shook his head, looking as though he couldn't believe what he had just heard. Bull was as expressionless as ever. No sign must be given than that he was anything less than menacing.

'Tell us about this man,' I said.

'I don't know his name, but he was Chinese, I think. We have Chinese come for safaris from time to time. Short, fat, dark hair. That's as much as I can remember. I thought I might have seen him before — maybe a previous safari — but I'm not sure.'

A previous visit? That would make sense. Scope out the land. When you're thorough, there's less chance of things going wrong, of being caught and punished. Professionals? Probably. Stan would have done a better job of things, though.

'What happened this morning?' I said.

'I told them you would be at the west fence, and the man said to stay away. That there were going to be bad things happening. I didn't know what he meant by "bad things", but I stayed away. I had the impala to skin and joint and then give some to the families in the village. There was work to do.'

'Where did you get the hand grenade that you used to kill the impala?'

'The man gave that to me. He said it was an easy way to kill a few impala or kudu or springbok all at one time. Said it was a gift.'

'Do you know how many men we killed today?' said Bull.

'No,' he said. 'I have heard nothing.'

'We killed seven,' Bull said, 'and the other three are currently in hospital. This is a deadly game and you should know the retribution it brings. Retribution? Getting what every-one deserves. And they all lived unhappily ever after. Phone Munroe, Pieter, and tell him what we have found out. Tell him to bring an ambulance, too, but he will probably guess that. I can almost hear him groan from here.'

We stood over Banti so that he wouldn't try to escape again, but there was little chance of that, given that there were three of us and he had two bullets in his leg. Tends to slow one down. Doesn't do any harm to be cautious, though. By now, the adrenaline would have stopped pumping and the leg wounds would be painful.

'Twice in one day,' Munroe said. 'Are you on a productivity bonus, Silver? Still, at least there are no corpses this time. What do you have for me?'

'His name is Banti, and he's been working for the poachers, telling them our movements so they could evade us,' said Pieter. 'Poaching a bit on the side for his own good, too.'

'You might be able to get something out of him,' I said. 'He says his contact is Chinese. That would fit with the victims of this morning's action. Are you allowed to sweat him?'

'Wouldn't do any good,' said Munroe. 'The poachers will either pay him to keep quiet or they'll threaten his family. Either way, he won't talk.'

'So this has been for nothing?' Bull said.

'You've smoked out your spy,' Munroe said. 'Made life more difficult for the poachers. Don't reckon it will put them off. The prize is too big. You've seen the poverty here. They could hire the services of every man in the whole village if they wanted to. Do you really think you can win against them?'

'We're not doing too bad,' I said. 'If we keep picking them off, they might back off and go somewhere else.'

'Kicking the can down the road,' Munroe said. 'Net result? Nothing.'

'I've got someone working on a plan,' I said. 'We'll take them down. We don't quit.'

'Should I know about this plan?' he said.

'Probably best not to,' Bull said.

'Does this plan involve an armoury of guns?'

'Knives, too,' Bull said. 'We don't like to be typecast. We call it flexibility.'

'Some might call it a bloodbath,' Munroe said.

'Everyone's entitled to their view,' said Bull.

Munroe laughed and shook his head. 'You guys get me,' he said. 'You're from a time that doesn't exist anymore. The age of chivalry is dead. You don't have to be sitting at a round table working out how to get the Holy Grail.'

'Someone's got to do it,' I said, 'and we seem to be the only game in town.'

'You know Arthur's knights failed? They never found the Grail.'

'But they kept trying,' I said. 'They kept trying. If it's all the same to you, we'll get going. Banti, keys to the jeep?'

'Table by the door.' He winced. 'Where's that ambulance?'

I scooped up the keys and turned round to face Munroe. 'It's been good to know you,' I said. 'Now might be a good time for that holiday you've been promising yourself, or maybe keep a low profile for a while. There's going to be a lot happening that creates a lot of paperwork.'

'Don't give me a reason to arrest you,' he said. 'I will if I have to. When it comes to the law, there's no exception for friends. Make sure they shoot first.'

As Bull and I got into Banti's jeep, Pieter drove off in his, anxious to get every minute before the arrival of the guests. I got into the driving seat and turned to Bull. 'What do you make of that?'

'Munroe won't cut us any slack,' he said. 'We've been useful so far, but if it comes to breaking the law, we're in trouble.'

'And we've got to break the law to achieve our ending. I hope Stan comes up with a good plan.'

'Me, too, brother,' Bull said. 'Me, too. Or we're in deep trouble.'

'As ever.'

CHAPTER NINE

Penelope was up and about when we got back. She still didn't look quite back to normal — whatever normal was for her, which was a frightening thought — and I didn't think the martini she was drinking would help matters. Someone's definition of madness: doing the same thing over and over again and expecting a different result.

Pieter was pacing around, so Bull and I went to join Red and Stan at our usual table. Within a nanosecond, Ibo brought us beers and the day seemed even better.

'Mission accomplished?' Stan said.

I nodded. 'Even better than expected. Bull got in some shooting practice, too.'

'Good to get it all out of your system by firing a bullet or two,' Red said.

'Took me two bullets when it should have been only one,' Bull said. 'I put it down to lack of beer.'

'Lack of beer's got a lot to answer for,' said Red.

To prove it, we sipped.

A small bus pulled into the camp and sixteen weary passengers got out. There was a melange of ages and styles of dress, reflecting an eclectic mixture of nations. The Americans were easy to identify due to the knee-length shorts and eye-dazzling shirts of the men. Pieter guided them to tables, and Ibo moved among them with glasses of refreshing orange juice — no alcohol yet. That was timed for when they had unpacked and they could watch the sun go down.

Pieter stood at the front of the group and clapped his hands.

'Guests,' he said. 'Honoured guests. My name is Pieter and I welcome you to a safari that takes you up close to the wildlife of South Africa. This, I hope, will be the experience of a lifetime.'

I hoped it wasn't one where bullets were flying around and they needed to take shelter in the stockade we had built. Animals, yes. Bullets, no.

'We're going to start off slowly,' Pieter continued. 'Give you a chance to get acclimatised and to adjust to our time zone. Tomorrow morning, we will take things easy with a drive by open-top bus. The next few days after that, we will be staying at two camps in the middle of the wildlife. There is one next to a waterhole and one by a river. The emphasis will be on living like the olden days. Our marvellous chef, Munty—' She took a bow — 'will be cooking you some of the famed dishes of South Africa. Our rangers, Ranu, Ackta and Smarfy—' They stood as their names were mentioned — 'will be helping to serve you and give you one of the staples of South Africa, a braai — a barbecue. You will eat dishes you won't have tasted before — impala, kudu and boerewors, for example.

'The temperature gets high here, so we will begin each day just after dawn, when it is cooler and the animals are not hiding away from the sun. We'll finish each day's sightseeing with a drink and watching the sun go down. In the evenings, we will sit around a campfire reliving the day, swapping stories and gazing at the myriad of stars in the night sky. You don't need to worry about malaria — South Africa is malaria-free. You will need sun creams and a spray to put off the insects:

if you've forgotten to pack any of those, we have some in the office. Your safety is our first priority. Our rangers, armed as you see, will accompany us at all times, including guarding you throughout the night. Both camps are protected by electric defences to keep out the animals. You can relax and enjoy the vista of South Africa.

'Two things I'd like to add. Firstly, let me introduce you to Penelope. She came on the last safari we did and enjoyed it so much she has come again. She might be able to tell you the answers to any questions you might have. She's here on her own, so make her feel like a friend.

'Secondly, we are privileged to have been chosen by the South African Army to be part of a training exercise. You'll see a lot of Johnny, Red, Stan and Bull—' He pointed to us — 'and a lot of weapons. No need to be alarmed. They'll be giving us an even higher degree of safety. So, my friends, relax and enjoy every minute of your time with us.

'Oh, one last thing,' he said. 'One of our soldiers, Red, is half Texan and half Comanche. He'd like to do a Comanche ritual for us for a good time this week. Come forward, Red.'

Of all the ways to die, I hadn't figured it would be by embarrassment.

Red moved near Pieter and started humming and stamping his feet. He did the trick he had used with the elephants, hands up, two fingers raised on each, and swept around the circle of guests. Finally, two minutes after he had started — which was two minutes too long — he made a cry to the heavens and bowed.

There was a polite burst of clapping, and Pieter led them to their tents.

Red returned. 'Good, hey?'

'Let's not discuss it, Red,' Stan said. 'I am speechless.'

There was a moment of silence, then we moved on seamlessly or some such.

'I hope Pieter's shooting is better than his speech-making,' said Bull. 'He didn't explain about the shower and toilet

95

facilities. There's going to be some disappointed people come sunrise.'

'It's all about communing with nature,' I said. 'For me, I wouldn't fork out hard-earned money for it, but you have to cater for all tastes, however strange they are. Did you notice how old some of these people are? The average age must be over seventy. I've seen two men with sticks — I wonder how they will manage for the walking part of the safaris.'

The guests started to filter back and take seats, forced to mingle by the formation of the tables. Pieter had set one up near Munty's kitchen. It was fully stocked with bottles of liquor and mixers, red wine opened to breathe and white wine in buckets of ice. The guests could either help themselves or get Ibo to take their order and serve it at the table. All wishes covered, as we would say in the language of mercenaries.

We started to wind down, but not for long.

A pair of guests approached us.

'May we join you?' the man said.

'We'd be delighted,' Stan said. 'Let me get you chairs.'

Stan moved two spare chairs from another table and set them around us.

The man was old. My guess would be eighty if a day. He was wearing shorts and a shirt that should be classed as a lethal weapon. If it got any louder, your eardrums would burst. He had on long white socks and penny loafers. He was American, I guessed. The woman looked younger, but only by, say, five years. She was wearing a long blue dress and was about five foot two. She had on three-inch heels, which I suspected she wouldn't wear again throughout the days ahead.

'Jesse,' the man said, 'and my wife is Joni.'

'Like Mitchell,' she said. 'You know, like the singer.'

I revised my guess of her age to around seventy. But she had good taste — that was important, if we were stuck with them for dinner.

'Is that a Kalashnikov?' he said. 'Been a while since I've seen one. I served in Vietnam, you know? Long time ago now.

96

Thank God. Brutal. Our men were raw, and the Cong were masters of jungle warfare.' He shook his head. 'Lots of guys didn't make it. I preferred the Colt M16. American-made, and so no problems that you got with the Kalashnikov — never jammed on you. With a Kalashnikov, you needed to always leave the bottom bullet hole empty to let the dust and crap settle in the bottom and make it less likely to jam.'

This was a man who knew his weapons. He rose up in my opinion. Maybe we'd spend the evening talking about guns, which would not be a lot of people's chosen topic of conversation. I imagined Joni must have heard it all many times before.

'You've got the monster sniper rifle and Hi-Powers in the holsters, as well. You guys aren't going to lose any battles for lack of weaponry.'

'I've got a sawn-off shotgun to add to the list, too,' said Red.

'Don't get him started,' said Joni, 'or we'll be here till this time next week.'

'Some stories just have to be told,' he said, 'so we don't forget, so we don't make the same mistakes in the future. Once you were in Vietnam, there was no going back. Your life changed, never to return to normality.'

'It was a long time ago, Jesse,' said Joni. 'These don't want to hear all your stories.'

'That's where you're wrong,' said Jesse. 'These guys don't fool me. They're as much South African Army as I am. Too many different backgrounds for the army to recruit, for starters. The regular army wouldn't issue these weapons. There's something going down, isn't there? I just want you to know if you need an extra pair of hands, I'm your man. You can count on good old Jesse.'

'Can you keep your mouth shut, Jesse?' I said, having realised there was no point in denying it. 'We don't want the guests to know who we are. It's important that no one is made to feel edgy.'

'Jesse don't tell tales,' he said.

'You're always telling stories,' said Joni. 'You'd bend the ears off anyone given half a chance.'

'But I know what to say and what not to say,' Jesse said. 'These guys can trust me.'

'Whose idea was it to come on this safari?' I said.

'It's been part of our bucket list for a long time now, but time is running out,' said Joni. 'Jesse's got the big C, the last fuel left in his tank. We have to pack a lot into life now, while we still can. We chose this safari because it promised to be an experience of a lifetime. Something never to forget. At least, it might give Jesse something else to talk about other than Vietnam.'

'Does the camping out and basic facilities not cause you any concern?' said Red. 'Do you not worry about things like the shower needing buckets of water? Us Comanches can sleep under the stars, if there's no other option, but the rest of you . . . ?'

'As I said,' Joni said, 'experience of a lifetime. Could be a disaster, but it might just be fun. What's to risk?'

'It's poachers, isn't it?' said Jesse. 'That's why you're here, isn't it? No other explanation.'

'You're too smart for us, Jesse,' Bull said.

'You guys gonna be at the campfire tonight?' Jesse said.

'Some of us will be there,' said Stan. 'The rest of us will have other things to do.'

'Guard duty?'

You couldn't fool this guy. It might be good for the general atmosphere if we kept them as far away from the other guests as possible. Get them to join us for meals and around the campfire. Somehow, though, Jesse didn't seem the sort of man who'd go blabbing.

'Get yourself a drink,' I said. 'We'll pull up another table and you can join us to watch the sun go down. You won't be disappointed by the spectacle.'

'We've got a special bottle of Polish vodka, if you're in the market,' said Stan.

'Bourbon man myself,' Jesse said. 'Always drunk bourbon, and don't see any reason to change now. Thanks for the offer, though. Takes a kind man to share anything special.'

They went over to the drinks table and Red went to get more cold beers. Ibo seemed to be doing well at swiftly keeping the guests happy. The omens were good.

Stan dragged up an empty table, courtesy of there being only sixteen guests, and we sipped beer as the sun dipped down on the horizon.

Jesse and Joni returned, Jesse with his bourbon on ice and Joni with a dry martini mixed by Ibo. Powerful stuff. I hoped she wouldn't succumb like Penelope, but she didn't seem the dipso type.

'How old's the boy?' asked Joni.

'He's fourteen,' I said, 'but mature already.'

'What're the prospects around here?' said Jesse.

This was Stan territory. He'd have researched everything before we set foot in the country. Didn't leave anything to chance.

'Unemployment is high,' said Stan, 'together with crime and corruption. Failed government investment and collapsing infrastructure add to the list. Many reckon that South Africa is a failed state. Opportunities for boys like Ibo are virtually non-existent. Too many people chasing too few jobs. The economy is reliant on tourism. Over half the people are living in poverty. Bad shape, all round.'

'Anything people like us can do?' said Joni.

'Just keep coming,' I said. 'Recommend to all your friends.'

There was a moment of silence.

'Wow. Look at that sky, Jesse,' she said. 'You don't get a sky like that in Texas. Worth all the money we paid, just for that.'

'Low pollution,' said Stan. 'Makes everything clearer. You'll notice it when the dark comes. Stars are brighter.'

'How's the bourbon?' I asked.

'Favourite brand,' he said. 'Whoever chooses it knows his business.'

'And the dry martini, Joni?'

'Fantastic,' she said. 'You couldn't have too many of these, or you'd fall to the floor.'

Well said. Sensible lady.

'Ain't too many things that are better than Texas,' Jesse said,' but this sky is to die for . . . or maybe I could have said that better.'

'Ain't afraid of dying,' Bull said. 'It's the manner of it that scares me.'

'Die with a gun in your hand, eh?' Jesse said. 'Go with dignity. I'm with you there.'

'This is all getting a bit morbid for the time of day,' I said. 'Sort of conversation that is more suited to having around the campfire. Joni, tell us what you do.'

'Used to be in real estate,' she said. 'Thanks to Jesse, didn't need the money, just something to do during the days. Rich beyond the dreams of Alice — isn't that what they?'

'I think it's avarice,' I said, 'but I get the picture.'

'I mainly do charity things now,' she said. 'Hosting lunches, auctions with dinner. Lady of leisure, I suppose you could say. I help with my grand-nephews and grand-nieces at times during the week — give their parents a break. Grown too old for getting down on the floor playing with trains and such. Not too old for reading stories, though. I make some up, too. People reckon that I should write some down. Maybe see if I could get them published, but I reckon they're just saying that to make me feel good. Eight kids in all. I'll show you some pictures at dinner. What's the food like?'

'Munty is a marvel,' I said. 'You won't believe what she comes up with in that tiny kitchen. The meals are mainly meat-based — plenty of that in South Africa, mostly beef — the round sausages have to be ninety per cent meat, for example. And then, of course, there's game — impala, kudu, springbok, that sort of thing, even crocodile from time to time. You'll certainly be trying some unique dishes.'

'What's the beef like, Red?' Jesse said. 'As good as Texas?'

'Nothing could be as good as Texas,' Red said.

'You said it!' said Jesse. 'The barbecue sure smells good. Let's try it.'

We left the table and formed part of the small queue outside the kitchen. Springbok was today's game. I wondered if Munty had played another trick on Penelope — told her it was impala, just for a laugh. Going with the springbok was a bowl of Roosterkoek, a barbecued bread with cheese, tomatoes, red onions and chutney and another bowl of green beans. Munty could keep the food industry of the country safe all by herself.

Pieter came over to speak to us while we were waiting. 'How's it going, guys? Sir? Madam?'

'Can't be faulted,' said Jesse. 'You run a tight ship here. Things may be tricky getting up in the middle of the night to use the restroom, and I do that frequently, but that seems like a small price to pay. You've certainly got the security problems covered. Great bunch of guys to have guarding you, whether it's lions or bandits.'

'Pieter's a part of our group,' I said. 'You can bare your soul with him. But not in public.'

'What's your availability, Pieter?' I said. 'Although I can hazard a guess.'

'I feel obliged to stay with Penelope,' he said. 'It can feel lonely here on your own.'

'There's sixteen other guests here,' I said. 'Plenty of opportunity to pal up with them. I thought it was all about the safari experience. Making new friends is a part of that.'

'I'll pitch in tomorrow on the game drive,' he said. 'Make up on what I've not contributed so far.'

'Can I have that in writing?' said Bull.

'Must fly,' Pieter said. 'Mingle, mingle, mingle.' He crossed the room to join a small group of smartly dressed Scandinavians.

'Did I detect a note of tension?' Jesse said. 'I get the impression that Pieter ain't pulling his weight.'

'He'll come right,' I said. 'We can cut him some slack for a while. He'll have a part to play before this adventure is over. I sense that.'

We returned to our table and Joni dipped into her bag and took out her phone. 'I promised you some pictures of my grand-nephews and nieces, and I always keep my promises.'

'Only thing to do with promises,' Bull said. 'No point in them, otherwise.'

'You guys talk my kind of language,' said Jesse. 'Do you hold honour dear, too?'

'You don't need to ask,' Bull said. 'A person's got to have principles to live by.'

'Maybe we'll look at the pictures when we've finished our springbok,' Joni said. 'Can't let the food get cold after all the effort Munty must have put in.'

'Meat's good,' said Jesse, after the first bite. 'I can't put my finger on it — like chicken with a stronger flavour. Like lamb, but more subtle.'

We were silent for a while, enjoying the food and the new experience of flavours not found elsewhere. We watched Pieter light the campfire, ready for the last hours before guests would start going to bed for an early start.

When we had finished, Jesse said, 'I'm a little disappointed that no one has asked me what I used to do before I retired.'

'Don't have to,' Red said. 'You're from Texas, and what's the biggest money-maker in Texas? Oil. Am I right?'

'You got it. Lucky strike. We were drilling for a new source of water on the ranch when it started to fill up with oil. Life changed in that moment. And here we are now, eating springbok with a glass of decent red wine under the stars. Who'd have thought it?'

'Do you believe in fate?' I said.

'Never thought of it,' said Jesse.

'I think everything is destined to happen,' I said. 'What proof have I? Can you think of a world without Joni? Impossible. You were always destined to meet Joni at some time or by some twist of fate. Right, let's see those photos, Joni.'

We politely looked at a show reel of pictures. Joni never mentioned the reason she and Jesse didn't have grandchildren,

102

and we never asked. Clearly, Joni was proud of her surrogate grandkids, and loved them very much.

Then it was time to meet up at the campfire. 'You guys get going,' I said. 'I'll take first watch. Jesse and I can swap some stories around the fire.'

'I'll see you in two hours,' said Bull. 'Save some stories for me, Jesse.'

They took one of the jeeps and headed out to the first camp. Jesse and I went to the fire, and Pieter put some more logs on to see us through the night.

'You know what else gives you away?' said Jesse. 'The eyes. You all have steel in your eyes. The eyes say, "Don't take a chance on me." You've killed many people, I would guess, and wouldn't shy away from doing so again, if the circumstances warranted it.'

'Good judgement,' I said. 'What makes us harder to defeat? It's being a group. We support one another. We are greater than the sum of our parts. We killed some people this morning. They were poachers. They were bad men. They'd kill an elephant for its tusks, and anybody that gets in their way. You'll see an elephant at some stage of the safari, and you'll see why they are precious and must be protected. We only kill bad men. We have our principles, like Bull said earlier. We've never killed an innocent man, or without giving the bad guys a chance to repent and lay down their arms.'

The fire glowed yellow, and Jesse and I stared into it, hoping to sort out the troubles in the world.

'How long have you got, Jesse?' I asked.

'A year, maybe a bit more. That's why I'm gonna enjoy this safari to the full. Seize the day. Isn't that what they say? Make every day a special one. Oh, enough about me. Tell me about this Pieter guy.'

'Let's put it in context,' I said. 'None of the five of us needs to work: Stan's got a hotel by a lake in his native Poland; Red's got a ranch in Texas that he won at a game of poker — a ranch with mineral rights that won't give out till long after his death. Bull runs boat tours that offer the chance to catch big fish off the Caribbean island of St Jude; I run a beach bar there, too. I'm also one of the heirs to the family investment bank, Silvers. All of us earned enough to live in splendour after a job we did in Amsterdam. Pieter runs this safari trip. He shouldn't be on the rocks. His problems would be few if it wasn't for poachers. We're here to solve that problem. There's nothing we wouldn't do for a friend. He's a man for the ladies and, here and now, it is tricky. Some people would say it's karma. He must have captivated the heart of Penelope. I suspect she has ideas of a wedding — after the divorce, that is. He feels he has obligations towards her, but he'll be lucky if he can resolve this situation without hurting her feelings. At the end of the day, he will be back to us and the job we're doing for him.'

'And tomorrow?' said Jesse.

'Tomorrow's for the lady called Fate,' I said. 'Maybe tomorrow, or the days after that, we will spin the roulette wheel where black is life and red is death. Who can tell? Right now, we're outnumbered with an enemy who could raise as many men as you could imagine at the toss of a coin. There's only one route out. The final battle. We're going to have to eliminate them. Which means we're going to have do a lot of killing. Fate decides the rest.'

'Is your name on the bullet?' Jesse said. 'Is that what you mean?'

'Precisely. That bourbon seems low in the glass, Jesse. Do you want to get another before you turn in?'

'You're an observant man,' he said. 'Keep my place.'

The camp was quiet apart from the soft voices of the few guests who hadn't gone to bed and the hum of the generator. Jesse returned with a glass in each hand. 'I got you a vodka over ice,' he said. 'I remembered you saying you guys had a liking for it. Don't like drinking alone. Won't be long before Bull comes to relieve you. One vodka can't do any harm. I imagine you could fire that Browning in your sleep.' He raised his glass. 'Here's looking at you, Johnny. Let's drink to tomorrow and what it brings. May you not be troubled.'

'Amen, Jesse,' I said. 'Amen.'

104

CHAPTER TEN

The guests assembled for the dawn drive. I imagined that the bus was a disappointment to some: to the rest, it was part of the simplicity of the adventure, the lure of the wild. I was carrying the Uzi, the dart gun and the sniper rifle with my trusted Browning Hi-Power in the holster. Pieter — with an assault rifle — and I supervised the boarding, and Ranu — dart gun — was joining the party, too. Smarfy was driving, and he would have a rifle on the front passenger seat of the bus. Plenty of guns if the action got tricky. Our final passenger was Ibo, to widen his experience. Bull and Stan were going on a reconnaissance trip to scope out the house of the opposition, and Red was on duty to safeguard the camp. All bases covered.

The plan was to cover the east side of the reserve today and part of the northern section tomorrow, when staying at the first camp. We would be running down to the sea, which would be a spectacular backdrop to the open plains of the reserve.

The first animals we came across were a herd of kudu with their spiral horns, which were so razor sharp that most predators avoided them. They were grazing on the lush grass of the savannah, where there was a good view all around of any approaching danger from predators. The guests snapped away on their phones and on digital cameras with a multitude of lenses and filters, equipment that seemed so plentiful we should have had a trailer to carry it all. They were never going to forget the trip, hopefully for the right reasons.

Along from the kudus were impala and springbok. They were agitated, feeding only in little bursts as they constantly looked around. It was almost like they could sense danger. Then we saw it.

A leopard crouched low and motionless, staring. It was eyeing the animals, looking for the easiest prey, the young or the lame. Suddenly, it charged into the impalas and chased a straggler. The impala was going to be too slow, and the only question was how long it would take before it was caught.

We were all spellbound by the chase. The leopard was strong, the impala swift, but not swift enough. The leopard brought it down and went for its neck, ripping into its flesh and squeezing the lifeblood from the beautiful impala. Yet the leopard was beautiful, too. A powerful killing machine. This was the game of life and death played out before us.

'I got it!' said Joni. 'The whole damn thing! I got it! A video of it all. Boy, I can dine out on this for the next year.'

'Good for you, Joni,' said Jesse. 'We can relive this moment for the rest of our lives.'

'Shame,' someone said. 'I was rooting for the impala.'

'The leopard's got to eat, too,' said Pieter. 'All part of the rich tapestry of life. If the leopard didn't kill the impala, the numbers would get out of control, and then there wouldn't be enough grass to feed them. Impalas would starve. Better to have a swift death at the hands of the leopard than to die slowly through starvation.'

'I'd go for that,' said Jesse. 'Better to die quickly than to linger on when there's no hope.'

There were reasons why Jesse would think that way, but I agreed with his sentiment. 'Die with a gun in your hand', wasn't that what he had said?

Pieter banged on the roof of the truck's cabin and Smarfy moved on.

Ranu shouted something at Pieter and pointed ahead. It was a plume of smoke. Someone had started a fire, and there was only one answer to who that was. The poachers.

Pieter immediately called the fire brigade. They were used to dealing with fires in the reserves. Most of the time, they would be deliberately started by the rangers in order to regenerate the land of dead wood and bring about regrowth — the green shoots of recovery, literally. At other times, like today, it would be arson.

'No need to be alarmed,' said Pieter. 'It will probably be a small fire and no risk to anyone. It's an old trick that poachers use as a diversion — resources have to go to fight the fire, giving the poachers a free run elsewhere.'

The smoke seemed to be getting thicker as we drove towards the west of the reserve, where we had fought the poachers the day before. We were about five minutes away when we saw the first flames among the trees where the elephants had appeared.

I saw no signs of wildlife. 'Where is everything?'

'Everything will head to the river,' Pieter said. 'They know they will be safe in the water. When this fire is under control, we'll go to the river and see everything in one go.'

'How long before the fire brigade gets here?' I said.

'They're unlikely to be busy, and they come fast to the reserve. They will go as fast as the terrain permits, which is slow. About another fifteen minutes is my guess. As long as there's little wind to spread the fire, they should put it out quickly.'

Pieter's guess turned out to be pessimistic. The fire engine appeared after only ten minutes, drove straight up to the trees where all the smoke was coming from and they started spraying. Soon, you could see the fire being stopped, the flames dwindling. The fire officers sprayed some more just to be on the safe side.

We all breathed a sigh of relief.

One of the fire officers came over to Pieter. 'How did it start?'

'Poachers,' Pieter said. 'A distraction would be my guess, or it could simply be a warning — show how much power they had. That they could do whatever they want to earn a hundred grand a time for a pair of tusks.'

'What are you going to do about it? You were lucky this time — no wind to fan the flames.'

'We're working on it,' Pieter said.

The fire officer looked at me. 'Would your solution happen to involve an assault rifle and a handgun in a holster? If so, you're going to have to get Captain Munroe on your side.'

'We're working on it,' Pieter repeated.

'I couldn't help seeing a lot of blood on the grass near the fence,' the fire officer said. 'Has your solution already started?'

'Like I said,' Pieter said, 'we're working on it.'

'Fight fire with fire,' I said. 'This act will not deflect us from stopping them in any way we want. No holds barred. It is a battle and we're going to win.'

'Mercenary?' the fire officer said. 'Am I right? I see it in your eyes.'

'This job is pro bono,' I said. 'There's others like me. We all have very edgy trigger fingers. We'll shoot first and ask questions later, of anyone who's still alive. Spread the word — this reserve is off limits for poaching.'

'I wish you well, Pieter,' he said. 'I hope you won't have to call us again. I have men who wouldn't say no to a bit of extra cash, if you need them.'

Pieter looked at me. I made a wave-like gesture with my hand. It meant I wasn't sure — see how things pan out.

'I'll bear that in mind,' Pieter told him.

The fire brigade left at a leisurely pace, taking in the wonders of nature, I guessed. It had been an interesting offer of help, and we could add that to our plans if necessary.

Pieter explained to the guests that they would change the itinerary to go to the river, where we might see more wildlife than they could have ever imagined. He banged on the roof and Smarfy got the truck moving.

The river was by the second camp, so we used that for the focus of our viewing. Pieter switched on the electric fence and everyone stood as near to it as possible.

The scene was magic. Lions in one group, prey in their own herds. The leopard was there. There was also a hippo in the water, in the basin that the river had made. I hadn't seen one on our previous tours of the reserve. It's strange — you could see a hippo in a zoo and it would look big, but it'd be at a distance from you. See it up close in real life and it appears absolutely enormous.

The guests clicked away to keep memories for posterity. Impalas, kudu and springbok were drinking gracefully and welcoming the brief respite that the water provided. And there it was — a herd of elephants drinking and hosing the water over themselves and their young through their trunks. A magnificent sight.

After a while, the animals drifted away, back to the reality of predators and prey. We travelled back in silence. Every guest was processing what they had seen. There were going to be a lot of celebrations tonight.

* * *

We were back after a long time at the first camp. Sundown was approaching and everyone was on a high. The atmosphere could only be described as electric. Ibo was working double on the drinks orders, but made time for us with a round of beers. Pieter made a short speech summing up the day and how well it had gone and went through the planned schedule for the morning and night at the first camp. This was where they would get down and get their hands dirty.

There was no stopping Jesse. 'I ain't one for public speaking,' he said, 'but I just have to say that what I have experienced today will live with me for ever. Although that might not be long, but that's another story. This tour has far exceeded my expectations. I could leave now and still have had value for money. Did you see those elephants? Did you see the lions? I can't wait till tomorrow. Now where's that bourbon, Ibo?'

There was a round of applause followed by chatter and laughs and, of course, the bourbon or such. We sat around the table not caring what Munty had cooked for us this evening and whether the red wine had had sufficient breathing time. This was what the perfect safari was all about.

'You seem to have had fun,' said Bull. 'I'm hoping the bar doesn't run out. There will be a few sore heads come the morning.'

'How did you guys get on?' I asked.

'The camp here was quiet,' said Red. 'Nothing to report. I spent some time with Munty while she was preparing tonight's meal. She's shunning a barbecue tonight, as that will be the order of the day when the rangers cook at the camps. Pieter is so lucky to have her. She keeps the engine functioning.'

'I've drawn up a plan of the house,' Stan said. 'I'll show it to you when we're alone for a while and we can study it.'

'And the basics?' I said. 'Can we get into the grounds and, if so, can we overcome whatever force there is in there?'

'We'll need blankets and steak and a length of rope with a grappling iron,' Stan said, 'and then we can get inside.'

'Blankets and steak and rope?' I said. 'I think I can see where the rope and grappling iron comes in, but the rest?'

'The walls are protected by barbed wire. We need to use the blankets to lay on top of it so that the spikes won't get us. The steak is for the dogs — we'll add some sedative to it for putting them asleep. The rope will be for us to climb over the walls.'

'Any idea how many men are there?'

'Hard to tell. There are a lot of vehicles, mostly jeeps, but that doesn't necessarily give us a count of men.'

'Stan and I reckon that they wouldn't need so many vehicles if they weren't going to be full,' Bull said. 'Our best bet is to put Ibo on watch there to monitor the comings and goings.

My guess is a lot, but they won't be trained fighters, just local tribesmen. We could either shoot them up or scare them so much they lay down their arms.'

'It will have to be done at night,' Stan said. 'There's no cover for us. It's all too exposed. Daytime would be out of the question.'

'They're renting the property,' I said. 'It might be useful to pay a trip to the estate agent who handled it. See if we can wangle a spare set of keys. Bribe, perhaps, or coerce them. It might be right up your street, Bull.'

'I'll take that as a compliment,' he said. 'Although I'm not sure if I should.'

'We all have our strengths.'

'And yours is?'

'Planning,' I said.

'I forgot about that,' Bull said, 'judging by how things usually pan out.'

'When has the plan ever gone astray?'

'Do you want examples in alphabetical order or by type?'

'You forgot chronologically.'

'A poor Jamaican boy like me wouldn't know what that meant.'

Jesse and Joni joined us before the banter became unproductive. They placed laden plates on the table, and it was our turn at the kitchen table now that the queue had died down. Munty told us it was called potjiekos, a beef stew with vegetables, and would fill us up after an exciting day and in preparation for the dawn patrol. Unsurprisingly, it was delicious.

Ibo, calmly but quickly, was touring the tables filling up the wine glasses and looking very happy. He'd had as much enjoyment out of the day as the guests. He must have learned a lot more about animals and about people. It would serve him well in days to come.

I looked around us. Smarfy, Ackta and Ranu were sitting on their own with plates of stew on their laps.

'What do you make of these guys?' I said.

'They're reliable in what they do,' Red said, 'but I wouldn't count on any of them in a fight. We need men who can kill if the situation demands it.'

'Killing animals is a good skill to have,' Bull said, 'but killing a man is a whole lot different. It has to be part of you. You can't teach it. You've either got that frame of mind or you haven't.'

I got up from the table and walked over to them. 'How are you guys? It's been a long, hard day. Can I get you a beer to show my appreciation?'

'We have to be guarding throughout the night,' Ranu said. 'We thank you for the gesture, but no.'

'We can cope with just two of you at the first camp, but I think we need to have one of you looking out from here. Can't have the back door vulnerable. Sort it out between yourselves. I'm planning that one of us will stay here, too. It would be good to have someone here as relief, to give the other person a break for a couple of hours.'

'Will do, sir,' Ranu said.

I was eating the stew when I had a thought.

'You've stopped eating,' Stan said. 'Don't like it?'

'No,' I said. 'It's fine. It's that I've just had a plan.'

Bull smacked his forehead with the heel of his hand. 'Not again.'

'But this time it's different.'

'In what way?' he said.

'This one might just work,' I said.

CHAPTER ELEVEN

There were some bleary eyes when the guests assembled by the bus in the morning. Bags — essentials only — had been packed into two of the jeeps along with meals and drink for the first night and sent off in advance to the first camp. A small bag, as instructed, was retained for the bus. Ibo was to stay at the base camp today, along with Stan on guard duty. A day with Stan, our tactician, might teach the lad a lot about thinking and decision-making. No minute was ever wasted with Stan. Ackta was to be on the bus today and Smarfy would be our driver. Ranu was to remain. Bull was detailed to see an estate agent and would support Stan afterward. Everything seemed sufficient given our limited resources.

There was some encouraging tension between Pieter and Penelope that I hoped I'd learn more about at some time during the day. Might not be long until we could get him back in the fold.

Red and I climbed aboard and listened to Pieter give the same speech as the previous day. He banged on the roof of the driver's cabin and we were off. The air was cool and blew away some cobwebs from those who had had partaken too much the night before. We passed the first camp and dropped off Smarfy to make the final preparations for the night.

From there, we drove northwards and then headed east on a trail. The land was savannah fringed by hilly areas of trees. Giraffes were already gorging on the leaves. They regarded us with curiosity but no fear. I would have been happier if they had headed away — made life as difficult as possible for the trophy hunters, although you would need a pretty tall house to mount a giraffe's head.

It seemed to me, judging by their reactions to the giraffe, that some of the guests had grown a little blasé. They had got used to thrills, and it was consequently a little tame to see the same animals again.

And then it changed.

A herd of kudu was grazing on the lush grass when there was a flicker of movement from the surrounding trees. Pieter banged on the cabin to give the signal for Smarfy to stop.

'There,' he said. 'Three lionesses. They are forming a pincer movement. Soon they will strike. Get your cameras rolling.'

I spotted one of the lionesses against the cover of the trees. It was directly in front of me. Straining my eyes, I saw another two — one to the left and one to the right.

The middle one broke cover and charged at the kudu. The other two moved in the front and back of the herd, pinning them down. There was no escape. The only doubt concerned which of the kudu would be targeted.

The lionesses were clever. The main attack was to the rear of the chosen kudu — the part where the sharp tips of the horns were ineffective. Kudu horns could do a lot of damage, I reckoned. You don't mess one-to-one with a kudu.

The scene was set. The atmosphere in the bus was again electric. A stunned silence for what was being played out in the front of the guests.

'Come on, kudu!' someone shouted. The sentiment spread. 'Come on, come on,' became the chant.

Outnumbered and flanked, the kudu had only one course of action — to run as fast as it could. If it could outmanoeuvre the lioness in front, it stood a chance.

It ran straight at the lead lioness with his horns down and at the very last moment jinked to the left in a movement a top-class striker would do against a defender.

It was free.

The guests started to breathe again. Once in a lifetime, once more.

Pieter announced more of the details for the day. We were told that the bus would go to the furthest point east of the reserve and see a spectacular sight. After that, we would go to the first camp, viewing the wildlife slowly on the return and then at the waterhole for more photographs. The lionesses would go hungry today unless their luck changed. No one was upset about that.

We moved on at speed until we saw it. The Indian Ocean. Amazing! The contrast to the unbroken expanse of the savannah was truly spectacular. The track led us to a clifftop that overlooked the water. Some small steps had been cut into the cliff, widening the narrow feature of the land and zigzagging down to keep the slope shallow. Someone had fixed a rope that you could hold on to. Pieter led the guests, together with their small bags, down the steps with Ackta following.

Red and I took a path at the very top and the three of us were watching for anything coming up behind. We were kitted out as usual, with each of us having an assault rifle: the dart guns were left on the bus. I was happy that nothing could surprise us.

At the bottom of the cliff was a long beach of golden sand stretching as far as you could see. The sky was light blue with not a cloud in sight, and the contrast with the gold of the beach was worth a dozen pictures. There was not a soul to be seen.

'Ladies and gentlemen,' Pieter announced, 'now is the time to experience another moment of a lifetime — a swim in the Indian Ocean. Change into your swimming costumes behind your towels. Ladies to the north and gentlemen to the south. The water will be warm at this time of year. Enjoy.'

'You know something about the Comanches?' Red said. 'Remember? It's that we can't swim. We're landlocked. No reason to learn. This place makes me edgy.'

A few of the men, including Jesse, declined the offer to swim and they stayed back with us, politely facing the cliff, where we would see nothing if the towels happened to fall in what was a tricky operation if you've ever tried it.

We heard splashes and turned round to see everyone in the water.

'What do you think of this, Johnny?' Jesse said. 'You can't describe a sight like this.'

'Nothing like what I had thought to see on a safari,' I said. 'This has a special feel to it. Like it's a privilege to experience it and we have been granted that wish.'

'Joni's having the time of her life,' he said. 'I'd better take some pictures. Is that a seal I can see in the water?'

'Looks like that to me,' I said. 'I can see another two frolicking about.'

'This just gets better and better,' he said.

Then I was back in the reality of this world. I felt uneasy. We were too exposed, with the four of us with guns leaving our post at the clifftop and not protecting the bus. There could be lions at one side or poachers to the other.

I signalled to Red and we climbed back up, pausing at the top to scan for any dangers. It seemed all clear. We had been lucky. I vowed I wouldn't make that mistake again.

Refreshed after half an hour of swimming, the guests made their way up the steps and on to the bus. I thought about the night ahead and my heart sank. I prayed that tonight's barbecue wouldn't be kudu.

We cruised slowly past impala, kudu, springbok and their predators, lions, cheetahs and leopards, as well as scavengers — hyenas and wild dogs. It was almost sensory overload.

When we got back to the first camp, Ackta had arranged stackable chairs and wooden slabs in lieu of tables: meals on laps would be the order of the day. The smell of the barbecue was mouthwatering. My stomach rumbled and Red and I passed the time till dinner with a beer or two. The sun was getting low in the sky as the guests settled down in their tents and then appeared for a pre-dinner drink.

The activity at the waterhole ramped up as predator and prey drank together. The guests stood by the electric fence and sipped. I don't think many of them thought that such an experience as they had had today was possible. The meat on the barbecue was springbok, which was some relief, but I wondered how many of the guests would become vegetarian after this trip.

As the temperature dropped under the cloudless sky, Pieter lit a big fire, not only to keep us warm but to act as a deterrent for wild animals.

There was a general warmth in the gathering. It was unreal.

Jesse and Joni came up to Red and I, drinks in hands. Jesse had his usual bourbon — no ice, unfortunately, but there had to be some concessions made for such a day. Joni had a glass of red wine — warm white wine should never be allowed on this planet.

'You missed the swim today, Jesse,' I said. 'Any regrets?'

'Drowning is such a hard way to lose your life,' he said. 'Takes too long and has no honour. I guess you two can understand that. I'd rather die from a bullet, even if it's after putting one in my own skull.'

'Don't be so morbid, Jesse,' said Joni. 'Surrounded by such beauty, you shouldn't be so melancholy.' She touched his hand and squeezed it. 'The only bad way to die is to not be loved. That won't be the way for you.'

'Are we safe here?' said Jesse.

'What I understand from Pieter is that they've been doing these camp stopovers for years and there's never been any trouble.' I omitted my fears about the vulnerability of our group. 'You'll have the rangers on shifts during the night, and Red and I will do the same. Nothing will get past the fence and those of us on guard. Relax. We've got you covered.'

'I liked the support today for that kudu,' he said. 'It's a very British thing to do, isn't it, always favouring the underdog? I'm not sure we Americans would do the same. We're much more pragmatic. Like Pieter said, the leopard has to eat, too. What do you think, Red? You sort of have a foot in both camps.'

'The Comanches think of it like this,' Red said. 'The buffalo was sent to us by Manitou, our god. We eat it to sustain ourselves, we wear its hide to keep us warm and make our moccasins. It's all part of the magic that surrounds us. Kill only what you need. Never kill for pleasure. Respect the land and what it gives us. It's all part of the glorious circle of life.'

'Kill only what you need,' said Jesse. 'Will that be how you tackle the poachers? Kill only those that oppose you?'

'I would hope there will not be the need for anyone to die,' I said, 'but the poachers seem insistent. They must feel that the prize of ivory is too rich to turn down. They will come for us and then clear the reserve of elephants at a hundred thousand pounds each. It's not something I have ever thought about getting involved in, but having seen the elephants and the rhino in the flesh has changed my thinking. What the poachers are doing is unforgivable. They must be stopped, and we seem to be the only game in town. The crisis will come to an end soon, and we can all go back home to our families. Hopefully.'

'Time to eat,' Jesse said. 'I can't do anything heavy on an empty stomach.'

I laughed. 'Come on, my friend, walk with me.' I put an arm around his shoulder and led him to the small queue for the barbecue.

'What do you think is out there?' He stared into the darkness of the night.

'Nothing we can't handle,' I said. 'It's pure magic out there. Nothing should detract from that.

'You know, Johnny?' he said, 'we never had a son, Joni and me. If we'd been privileged, I would have liked him to be like you. It's good to know right and wrong in life. Maybe that's the best thing to learn. Hell, I'm getting tearful. Joni would admonish me for that. There's only one thing that can cure it.'

'Another bourbon,' I said.

'You got it.'

We loaded our plates with springbok and a jacket potato that had been sitting on the barbecue since we got back. We stopped at the bar table and replenished our drinks, then back to Red and Joni, who were still chewing the fat about something from our conversation.

No fat on the springbok, that was for sure. 'What do you reckon?' I said to Jesse.

'If I could get a beef franchise here, I'd be an even richer man. Everything is either beef or tastes like it. I'm not saying I dislike the cuisine, but it does get a bit samey, even after just a couple of days.'

'It's like the Midas touch,' I said. 'Everything you touch turns to beef.'

'Could be worse,' said Jesse. 'Could be cauliflower.'

'You got it,' I said, mimicking his earlier phrase.

Red and Joni left us to get their dinner, and when they rejoined us, we were a group of four again.

'What about the fire this morning?' Joni said. 'Are we at risk here?'

'No,' I said. 'It was just a small one, used as a diversion. The poachers knew all our resources would be at the site of the fire, and they would gather elsewhere. They can't afford a big fire getting out of control, because that might destroy the elephants before they can get to them. I don't know whether they will try another diversionary tactic, but we've got them covered.'

'You've dealt with this sort of thing in the past?' Joni said.

'Many times,' I said, 'and I'm still here.'

She looked down at her springbok. 'Would you like this?' She pointed at the meat. 'I seem to have lost my appetite.'

'Understandable,' I said. 'Yes, I think I could manage that. We mercenaries have a big appetite.'

'I won't ask what for.'

'Very wise,' I said. 'How do you think you'll be able to sleep tonight? Pretty Spartan here. No luxuries.'

'I'm so dog tired I could sleep anywhere. The early starts get to you. I heard from Pieter that we don't have to get up so early tomorrow. The animals will be coming to us, rather than the other way round.'

'You all deserve a bit of time to relax,' I said. 'The water-hole and the animals it attracts will still be here whatever time you wake.'

'I don't know how that Lady Penelope has managed to do the trip twice. I'd be totally exhausted.'

'I'm sure exhaustion doesn't come into her thinking,' I said. 'Too wrapped up in other things.'

'She's got the hots for Pieter, hasn't she?' Joni said. 'I'm not sure this would be the life for me. I'd be worrying all the time whether he would come back at night. Be a great place if you wanted somewhere quiet to write a novel, but otherwise it would be lonely. Too quiet for me. I'd go stir crazy.'

'Love is a strange thing,' I said. 'Love conquers all. The rest is just background trivia.'

'If someone had asked me about the mindset of a mercenary, the word I would have come up with is "thug". You don't fit the bill.'

'I can be a thug when necessary,' I said, 'but I've got a heart of gold.'

'I never know when you are joshing me,' she said.

'Not this time,' I said. 'Let me prove it by getting you a top-up of your wine. I might even get one for myself. One beer and a glass of wine won't hurt.'

I put my plate on the grass and got drinks for Joni and me. The red wine was a claret lookalike, and had plenty of depth and a good level of warmth, which went well with sitting around the campfire. I regretted not being able to have more of it, but I had to think about being on guard for two-hour slots during the night. Red must have felt the same, sipping at his bottle of beer. He looked at me. 'First or second?'

'Neither,' I said.

He looked at me like I'd gone loco.

'I think it's about time that Pieter pulled his weight,' I said.

'Well said, brother,' Red said. 'I'll take third in that case.'

'So I'll take second,' I said. 'I have to phone Anna, once I've worked out the time difference between here and St Jude. I think if I call now it might be afternoon for Anna, which would fit well, although I'm not absolutely sure. I keep getting things confused whether we're forward or back. I'll leave it for the start of my shift.'

Before that, I needed a progress report from Bull. I walked to the campfire and found a quiet spot. '*Que pasa, amigo?*'

'*Nada,*' he replied, 'although I'm only saying that as it's the only word of Spanish I know.'

'So what's going down?'

'I've got a spare pair of keys to the poachers' house — one box ticked on Stan's spreadsheet.'

'Did you have to get heavy to get them?'

'I just stood in front of the estate agent. You know me, all sweetness and light.'

'So you did have to get heavy, then.'

'Just a tad, let's say. What else has been happening, you might ask if you were a mercenary who needs to prepare for a battle that might kill you? Stan spent the day with Ibo giving basic rules on writing and arithmetic. Tomorrow, I will drop Ibo off to count vehicle movements, so that we can get an idea of the numbers we might face, if it comes down to that final battle. He's a good kid. He's smart, but has had no proper education. I plan to rectify that. Your end?'

'All quiet on the eastern front,' I said. 'I'm not looking forward to guard duty. Anything could be lurking out there in the dark, waiting to pounce. I keep telling myself that Pieter knows best and has done these things in the past without incident, but I can't overcome my level of doubt. I would be happier if we could call it a day — the guests have seen all the animals on their list — and could do some more bus trips rather than overnight stops.'

'How's Red?' Bull asked.

'You know Red,' I said. 'Comanche stuff whenever he sees the glimmer of an opportunity to turn the conversation that way. He's cool, though, and not made any enemies — I think the guests like him in his homely way. He and I are doing some bonding with Jesse and Joni.'

'How's Jesse's health?' Bull said. 'Is he holding up?'

'No signs of frailty,' I said. 'He's having the whale of a time, made even better by seeing Joni enjoying everything so much. It was the right thing for them to do, coming on this trip. The memories will last her a lifetime after Jesse passes over. What are your plans for tomorrow?'

'Cleaning every gun I can find while I keep guard.'

'Good plan,' I said. 'You can never have too many guns. *Ciao.*'

'Whatever happened to the Spanish?' he said.

'Ran out of words,' I said.

'In that case, *arrivederci.*'

We broke the connection. I looked around the fire and saw Pieter sitting next to Penelope. I placed a hand on her shoulder. 'I have to drag Pieter away from you,' I said. 'I hope not to break his spell.'

He got up and I steered him toward the dark of the fence. 'We need to talk,' I said. 'In a moment, the guests will be going to bed, if you could call it a bed, but that's neither here nor there. Like the rangers, Red and I will be guarding on rotation. You need to do your share. I'm allocating you the first shift.'

'Penelope won't like being on her own.'

'I don't give an overripe fig for what Penelope likes.'

Which was a more polite euphemism than what I wanted to say, but the last thing on my mind if there was even the slightest chance of being overheard. I didn't want to sound like Joni's thug.

'Understand?' I said.

'Yes, Johnny,' he said. 'You can count on me. Penelope could join me, maybe.'

'As long as it doesn't distract you,' I said. 'I need to sleep soundly before my shift and not be awake wondering whether I can trust you to keep watch or not. You'll also do another shift before dawn when Red wakes you.'

'I didn't come armed,' he said. 'I didn't think I'd need it with all of you carrying weapons.'

'You can borrow my Uzi,' I said.

'I've never used an Uzi before,' he said.

'It's an automatic weapon, Pieter,' I said, holding back. 'It has a trigger. You just pull on the trigger and it shoots bad men. I'm keeping the Hi-Power handgun. There's no way I'm going unarmed in this situation. Which brings me to the second subject we need to discuss. You have to change your itinerary. We are far too vulnerable here. The poachers could wipe us out if they knew where we were, and they had a mind to. We've been lucky lately that they have not made more of an attack. They're cooking something up, and we have to change the schedule. No more night camps. The guests can have short trips in the bus, but we need to face the nights where the five of us — note five, because it includes you — are all together to defend the base camp.'

'But won't the guests be disappointed?' Pieter said.

'Maybe,' I said, 'but they will be alive. You've given them two wonderful days to remember for the rest of their lives. No one will forget any tiny bit of it. Do your job. No more risks. Go get yourself ready for duty. I'll hand over in thirty minutes. Be ready. Use the time to think.'

He walked back to Penelope and she stood up from the chair by the fire. He led her to their tent, and I heard her shout at him.

Tough. Time for Pieter to man up.

I called home and it took a while before Anna answered. Maybe it was before dawn and I had woken her.

'Have you got time to chat?' I said. 'What is the time where you are?'

'It's early afternoon,' she said, 'and it's the lull before the sundown trade. I would like to talk. I miss you and if I can't see you, hearing your voice is the best thing to have.'

'I miss you, too,' I said. 'It's been a heavy day here, so many new experiences. You know, the guests swam in the Indian Ocean today? Wildlife aplenty that you wouldn't believe.'

'Life here has been as laidback, as usual. I learned to make a new cocktail, though — the Airmail. Basically, a daiquiri topped up with champagne, making a long drink. Apparently, you can substitute mescal for the white rum, but we are short of that for some strange reason. Mescal? What the hell is that?'

'It's made from the agave plant and is like tequila. The big difference is that the best mescal has a worm inside the bottle. Not something I would try.'

'When are you coming back, Johnny? It's so lonely here without you.'

'Just another few days, darling, and it should all be over. I can't wait.'

'When you say it will all be over, are you keeping safe?'

'When have I ever been in danger?'

'All the time,' she said. 'Don't take any risks. I want you back in one piece, but even more important is that I want you back.'

So as not to worry her, I segued the conversation into more mundane topics: the kids, the bar trade, the weather. I had the feeling that she didn't buy any of that and that she was close to tears — this was the longest time we had ever been parted. I cut the call, both of us realising that some things were best left unsaid.

CHAPTER TWELVE

I was worried. It was all going too smoothly. How we'd survived not being attacked I didn't know. The poachers were cooking up something. I had the nasty feeling that this was the calm before the storm.

After a talk with Red, I had a chat with Pieter and told him firmly that we weren't prepared to carry on with the overnight camps. He had to agree to the changes to the itinerary or we would pull out, go back home and leave him to accommodate the poachers. He'd lose every elephant with tusks because the poachers would slaughter them all in their quest for ivory. It was an ultimatum — an offer he couldn't refuse.

He made a speech when everyone had finished a breakfast of bread, butter and strawberry jam washed down with coffee and were about to take their chairs over to the fence to start the day's watching. The plan was being changed to stop the overnight camps — the guests were told something like the weather was going to change for the worse.

Honestly, I thought the guests were relieved. They didn't want to spend another night in such Spartan conditions. They'd done it once, and that was a memory that they could recall and view back through rose-coloured glasses. The box that was marked 'intrepid' could be ticked.

I called Bull and told him about the change in plans and that we would all be back for a late lunch. He had dropped Ibo off and was cleaning guns. 'Everything hunky-dory' was his report. He'd send jeeps for the luggage, which should arrive by twelve.

There was chatter among the guests when they saw a herd of impala drinking from the waterhole. This morning was due to be a walk among the animals, but Pieter was aware that I wouldn't allow it. Viewing sitting down was as far as I would go in terms of danger.

I waited until eleven o'clock, when I thought it would be nine in London, and called my secretary at Silvers for an update. Nothing urgent, she said. A board meeting was scheduled for the following week and, as far as she could see, there was little that was contentious on the agenda.

I broke down the Uzi and reassembled it: it was something I could do, literally, with my eyes shut because of the number of times I had done it over the years. I did the same with the Browning Hi-Power and then made sure they had full magazines. Anyone that tried to get us now would face a volley of bullets. However, if an elephant, undeterred by the electric fence, came to see what we were and how we were trespassing on its land, it could stroll in and kill us all.

The time passed slowly and I spent a while working on my plan for eliminating the Chinese. It was daring, but I liked it a lot. I wondered if the poachers had heard the phrase 'Expect the unexpected'. I hoped not.

I instructed Smarfy and Ackta to break down two tents as accommodation for the four of us mercenaries to use back at base camp, and asked Smarfy to make me some more coffee in the meantime. I drank it as I pulled a chair next to the guests and looked at the animals that had come down to drink at the waterhole. I suspected the guests were starting to get bored and that nothing short of an elephant would make them gasp. That was the last thing I wanted to see.

The jeeps arrived just as I finished my third coffee. I was jumping by that time. We loaded the luggage and the tents aboard and started to assemble at the bus. I breathed a sigh of relief when we pulled away. We had not had an incident, and for that I was grateful.

I could smell bacon cooking when we arrived back. Wonderful. Munty made sandwiches and handed them out to us. She'd even added some homemade ketchup. We ate as if it was our last meal ever, which, hopefully, would not be the case.

Bull kept looking at his phone to make sure he hadn't missed a call from Ibo, who'd been told to call when he was ready to be picked up. Bull was edgy, and I suspected now would be the time when he regretted the decision to have Ibo sent on the mission.

Most of the guests retired to their tents for a nap after lunch. All was quiet. The four of us, now reunited, sipped a beer and talked about my plan and whether we had missed anything. It involved luck, but what didn't? It was as good as we could get.

I broke down the guns again — something to do with a purpose. I cleaned the Uzi so you could eat your dinner off it, which, judging by last night, could be a possibility. I cleaned the Hi-Power and then the sniper rifle. Everything was squeaky. I resisted breaking them down and assembling them again. Too OCD.

Jesse had declined a nap and came across to me. 'You comfortable with guns?' he said. 'You like 'em?'

'As long as I'm on the right end of the barrel,' I said.

'Was that always the case?'

'I've had to use a knife on occasions, but a bullet is far less messy. You don't get covered in blood with a gun.'

'Where have you served?' he said.

'Most places that have a war — which seems to be a whole lot of places — or whenever there's somebody or something to protect. Angola was a disaster, but we finally put that to rest. A lot of Eastern European countries that seemed to be splitting apart or coming back together again. Two years fighting with the Israeli army to start with. That's where I got a liking for the Uzi. The army there taught me to kill, and I did so many times. I don't regret any of it, because it was always someone trying to kill me. Them or me? Wasn't a hard decision.'

'Did you always have those steel eyes? Was it nature or nurture?'

'I think it's something that happened along the way. My half-brothers don't have it, so I'd go with nurture. You build from your experiences. Tell me about Vietnam.'

'Hell of a mess,' Jesse said. 'Should never have happened. I never understood why we were there and who exactly we were fighting. We were so unprepared for a jungle war. The use of napalm to destroy the forests and anyone in them was unforgivable. Kill everything and everybody, that seemed to be the only plan. And you know the worst thing? I missed the summer of love. That wonderful time when we could do everything. That bonding together. I met Joni at a demonstration, after I was demobbed, and we've been together since. Was it all due to fate or was that just coincidence?'

'I'd go for fate. There have been many times in my life when it could have taken a different direction. Yet here I am, guarding elephants. Who would have guessed it? I've not asked you before, but was it a conscious decision not to have children?'

'Wasn't possible,' he said. 'Joni had a problem — endo something or other — and it was never possible.'

'So the patriarchal line stops here?' I said.

'Who do I leave it to? That's a problem. I have a trust fund set up for the great-nieces and great-nephews so they're catered for. I don't want them to have all my money — they need to work for a living. Know any good charities?'

'I know one in the UK that could make very good use of some money. Getting kids off the streets and giving them some chances. It would benefit kids across the country who currently have no stability and no future. It's a long story, but it could make a difference to their lives.'

'Give me details and I'll make sure it gets a share. If you're involved, I'm happy.'

Jesse drifted off to get a bourbon, now with the luxury of being able to pour it over ice. I grabbed a cold beer and settled down to welcome sundown and the peace it would bring.

Still, Bull had heard nothing from Ibo.

'I'm going,' he said. 'I don't like silence, especially this one. Something's wrong. I can tell.'

And then the gate opened. It was Ibo. He ran to Bull and collapsed into his arms. He was shaking like a bartender making a good cocktail.

'Calm down, boy,' Bull said. 'You're safe here. I'll protect you. Take a moment and then tell me what's happened.'

'They must have seen me and wondered what I was doing there,' Ibo said. 'They marched me into the house and tied me to a chair. A man said he would do horrible things to me if I didn't talk. They said they'd start by cutting off a finger. I told them what I was doing, and then they asked me details about what we were doing. How many people we had, how many guns we had. I told them everything. I let you down. I'm so sorry.'

'Nothing to be sorry about,' said Bull. 'In your place, I would have done the same.'

'They let me go and drove me to the gate. They gave me this.' He took a piece of paper from his pocket and handed it to Bull. 'I don't know what it says.'

Bull unfolded the paper and read.

'We have been invited to a challenge,' he said. 'One final battle. The day after tomorrow, at dawn, at the west fence where we fought the other day. If we win, they move on. If they win, those of us surviving will go, never to come back.'

'Are we all agreed?' I said.

They all nodded. We accepted the challenge.

'Send a ranger to deliver our reply,' I said to Pieter.

And so it was. A chance to resolve everything and get back to some sense of normality. Win and we could go back to our families and friends.

Lose . . . ?

It wasn't worth thinking about the consequences. It was a calculated gamble.

CHAPTER THIRTEEN

We had little more than a day to prepare for the battle. It wouldn't be so easy this time. They knew our strength. They knew we had occupied the mountain slopes, and that had allowed us to attack them from front and rear. They wouldn't make that mistake again. The odds were against us, but we'd faced that many times in the past and come out of it alive.

'I have a plan,' I said.

There were no groans this time. This was very serious.

I outlined what I was thinking.

'Puts a lot on Red's shoulders,' Bull said.

'Comanches can take pressure,' Red said.

'Red,' I said, 'can you not mention Comanches again until this is all over? How about giving us the other half of you — the Texan side.'

'Texans can take pressure,' Red said.

I gave up.

'Stan, Red,' I said, 'go and reacquaint yourselves with the territory. Look at some new tactics and how we might deploy our forces. We have the three rangers, but we can't rely on them. We can't ask them to risk their lives, and I can't blame them if they decide not to get involved. The battle will probably be entirely dependent on us five. See if we can make anything of using the battle time to our advantage — can we do anything in the dark to attack their forces before they're ready for kick-off?'

'"*To win the war you must defeat the enemy's finest troops,*"' Bull said. 'Sun Tzu, remember? That seems to be our only option. We can't give in now, or everything we've done is for nothing. I'll go with your plan, risky though it is. We came here to do a job, and I don't like things that are not finished.'

'Whatever our final tactics,' I said, 'we can't leave this camp unguarded. I propose that Pieter remains here to guard the back door and protect the guests. That means we're effectively down to the remaining four of us to fight in the battle. We four have fought there before — that's our best formation. Pieter, how are things with Penelope? Is she likely to want unrestricted time with you? Can you keep her out of the equation, so that you can be focused solely on your guard duty?'

'I think I can keep her out of the action,' he said. 'Be good not to have her clinging to me for a while. Despite her ways — the way she treats Ibo for a start, the way she bosses people around — I'm getting fond of her. You know what I'm like with women. I've not been in this position before. Love 'em and leave 'em has always been my mantra. I'm still not sure how I feel or what I should do.'

'Why don't you start tonight? Get her to address Ibo by name and not by "boy". I'm sure everyone would welcome that. Get her to mingle more with the other guests, so that the five of us could have time as a group and chew the beef on the battle without being overheard.'

'Will do,' said Pieter. 'How about setting her up with Jesse and Joni?'

'I like them too much to do that to them. I think they'd like some time on their own, to digest everything that has happened since being here. There must be some other couple that she could get to know.'

I smelled the charcoal from the barbecue as it heated up. Soon it would be sundown and dinner.

'Stan, do the honours. One glass of vodka won't hurt. I'd rather have vodka inside me than a bullet, so let's see if it gives us any protection.'

Stan got up and went into the office. He returned with five tumblers with ice inside them and a bottle of the chilled vodka. He poured, and we sat there sipping so as to appreciate its complex flavours.

The sun got lower and seemed to bring a sense of calm over the camp. The guests were refreshed by the revised itinerary and were enjoying a sundowner — all was well in the world as far as they were concerned. For dinner tonight, spiral sausages were on the menu. I was sure the guests would welcome not having meat that they had seen gambolling about during the day.

Bull told Ibo to lie down for a while and get some sleep, but he appeared soon after to help serve dinner and drinks. He was a strong boy, and we were all proud of him. Jesse and Joni dined alone, and I could see them holding hands. From the outside, all seemed right with the world, but we knew it couldn't last.

'Now that we are back to five,' Stan said, 'we can reduce each stint on guard to an hour and a half. Pieter, you take first. Bull?'

'I'll take second,' he said. 'I want to be around till Ibo is asleep. I'd only worry about him otherwise.'

'Any preferences?' Stan said. 'I'd like to take last shift, because Red and I need to get out at dawn. See what the terrain looks like at the time the battle will start.'

'I'll take third,' I said.

'Fourth for me,' said Red. 'Then I'll keep you company, Stan. I don't sleep well before a battle. Might as well do something useful, like sitting with a friend.'

'Any role for the sniper rifle?' Stan said.

'If I can see a spark when someone shoots, I can fire,' I said. 'Not guaranteed to be a hit, but it might pin down those on the mountain or force them to give up their positions and join those on the ground. For the rest of the men, I'll try to pick off the leaders. The only drawback with the sniper rifle is that it's slow. It's not like spraying a hail of bullets from an assault rifle. Its effectiveness depends on how much time I'm given. The good news is that the sights are set for the range. Last time, I was shooting down from the mountain. This time, it's the other way round. Same distance, but in reverse.'

'Sausages are good,' said Bull. 'Perfectly cooked. Eat them up before they get cold.'

'Can you take some of the bags of sand, Stan?' I said. 'Build more firing positions? Two sets, this time.'

'No problem. It will mark out our defences to the opposition, but the benefit of protection outweighs that. This is all coming together. I'm beginning to like it.'

'Let's not get carried away,' I said. 'Still a lot of work to do. I'm off to get a little sleep. Wake me up in three hours' time, Bull.'

'Want to know what worries me about the poachers?' he said.

'Tell all,' I said.

'They're going to cheat.'

* * *

I slept fitfully before my shift, and not at all after it. I gave in and got up, dressing in my camouflage gear and placing the Hi-Power in the holster. Ready for anything. I paced the perimeter of the camp checking that the fences were still intact and that the electric wires had power.

I thought about calling Anna, but I had no fresh reassurances to give her on my safety. In fact, the situation had got worse since we last spoke. Silence was the better option. She'd only worry more.

Ibo was up and about, although a little sheepish. He made me a coffee, and I invited him to join me at the table.

'How are you feeling today?' I said.

'Ashamed,' he said. 'I should never have talked. I betrayed you all. How can you trust me again?'

'You're a fourteen-year-old kid,' I said. 'No one blames you. Don't beat yourself up. You never know quite what they would have done if you hadn't have talked. They might have simply got over a problem by killing you, and then where would we be?'

He nodded and conjured up the semblance of a smile.

'There may still be a part for you to play,' I said. 'Be prepared for that. Did you get an idea about their strength?'

'There were only two jeeps that left and came back. Four men in each. When they captured me, I saw three more jeeps and many men. Too many to count. There was a big room where they were all sitting around smoking. I recognised some as local tribesmen.'

'That's good,' I said. 'They will not be professionals like us. They will not be used to fighting. They will not be used to killing. They will panic under pressure. Good work. Now, go and help your mother. Tell her I like my eggs sunny side up.'

I sat there on my own, thinking. Soon I would face the fourth horseman. The pale rider. Death. In the past, Lady Luck had always been on my side. Would she desert me now?

CHAPTER FOURTEEN

'You might as well get the guests on the bus and out of our hair,' I said to Pieter. 'Take all three rangers. You should be fully armed. Take a walkie-talkie and alert us at the first sign of danger. The four of us will come to your aid. Make it a short trip. Avoid the western stretch. The poachers will be thinking about tomorrow — you shouldn't have any problems today.'

'The thing that you have to know about a plan,' Bull said, 'is when to give up and switch to something else.'

'Wise words, my friend. You may have to remind me of that tomorrow. Now, Pieter. Be back for lunch, and serve drinks when the guests get back. Plenty of drinks. Maybe Munty could put together some heavily alcoholic punch and make some substantial food. I want them all to have a siesta, so they're relaxed. They may well need it. From that point, they should be contained here and close to the stockade. After that, who knows?'

'We will,' said Bull.

'We'll know more when Stan and Red get back,' I said. 'It's an audacious plan, even if I do say so myself. They're amateurs and we're professionals. I think we can take advantage of that, through the overall strategy and the tactics we employ on the ground. They won't have the experience to deal with what we can dole out. They'll make mistakes. That will be their downfall.'

I saved a bit of the bread from my breakfast and walked outside the camp, pacing out until I was happy with the distance. I placed the bread on the branch of a tree, lay down and tucked the sniper rifle into my shoulder to avoid any kicking when I fired. I sighted the bread through the telescopic sights and fired one round.

I could see through the sights that I had just caught the bottom-right corner of the crust of the bread. I made a minute adjustment to the sight and fired again.

Bull's-eye.

I drew comfort from that. At least one part of the plan had a chance of coming together.

Bull was out running, to burn off some of the nervous energy, and I sat alone at the table drinking coffee.

Jesse came up. 'Mind if I join you? I wouldn't normally ask, but it looks like everybody has other things on their mind. I thought you might benefit from some company.'

'Please do.'

'It's coming, isn't it?' he said.

'I didn't think it was that obvious.'

'Only to a man who's seen military action. You learn a lot about human nature. You sense things more. When's it coming down?'

'Dawn tomorrow,' I said. 'We're just making the final preparations.'

'What do you think are your chances?'

'No better than evens,' I said. 'We'll be heavily outnumbered, but they aren't as finely trained as us. And we have a plan.'

'Which is?'

I outlined it to him.

'I think I might have to look up the definition of "crackpot". I reckon "no better than evens" is optimistic,' he said. 'I'd love to be there to watch. It's going to be some battle.'

'You're best off here looking after Joni,' I said. 'We'll leave Pieter here to guard you all, but the action will all be at the west fence. You should be safe.'

'Can I have a gun?' he said. 'Just in case. I'd feel safer if I had a gun.'

'We've got a spare Browning Hi-Power,' I said, 'but what would Joni feel about that? Any chance she would panic?'

'She's level-headed,' he said. 'She'd see it as a last resort. I keep a Colt at home to make us feel safe. Since Vietnam, my philosophy has been to cover myself. I'll tuck it into the back of my trousers, so none of the other guests can see it. It'll be a comfort. The Browning is a hell of a weapon, from what I know. I'd be reassured to have one.'

'Wait here.'

I went to the office and opened the gun rack, took out the Browning and loaded it. I stuck it in the waist of my trousers and walked back outside. 'Ready?'

He nodded. I passed the gun under the table. He took it and put it at the back of his trousers.

'It's fully loaded,' I said. 'Thirteen rounds. I always thought that it should have been twelve or fourteen, thirteen being an unlucky number, but maybe the designers weren't as superstitious as me. You'll never use all thirteen of the bullets. If you haven't got rid of the opposition by the third bullet, then you'll be dead.'

He nodded.

'One condition,' I said. 'No heroics, understood? That's what the five of us are here to do.'

'Yes, Sergeant,' he said. 'Understood.'

'You'll have a small tour on the bus this morning and back in time for lunch. You'd be best not to dine with us at lunch or dinner. We won't be good company. Our thoughts will be elsewhere. By this time tomorrow, it will all be over, for better or worse.'

'Do you know why you are doing this? Risking your lives?'

'We made a promise to an old friend and, though he hasn't shown as much gratitude as I would have hoped, a promise needs to be kept. He's helped us in the past — fought with us side by side when we were in need — and we feel it is a matter of honour to help him now. If we walked away now, I would be ashamed of my conduct and always regret it.'

'Don't doubt him,' Jesse said. 'It's always tricky to refuse a lady. Penelope has got her claws in him, and it's hard for him to say no. It may be a matter of honour for him, too. He is feeling the weight of that honour, making him go with whatever she wants. And, I suspect, we haven't seen the good side of her yet. Maybe you should give her the benefit of the doubt.'

'If things go badly tomorrow, look after her. I believe she truly loves Pieter and will be devastated if anything happens to him. She has a good motive, but it just comes out the wrong way.'

'Let me get you another coffee.' He walked over to Munty and came back with two mugs. He passed one to me.

'I put in a little bit of brandy in it,' he said. 'Make this your last proper drink before tomorrow. I want your reflexes to be fully functioning when you fight. Whatever we say about "one drink won't do any harm", it does affect your speed of reaction. Ride on adrenaline tomorrow, not on alcohol.'

I picked up my coffee and toasted him.

'Cheers,' we both said. 'To tomorrow.'

* * *

Red and Stan came back just before lunch. We sat around with a jug of iced water and five glasses that we approached without much enthusiasm. It was business now. Just business.

'Report, please, Stan,' I said. 'Will it work?'

'We have to be there, ready, before them,' Stan said. 'If we arrive after them, they could pick us off before we get to the shooting positions. We're exposed up to that point. Pieter, you're going to have to do guard duty here tonight and through the morning. The four of us will have to spend the night there. You're on your own.'

'I can handle that,' Pieter said. 'You can rely on me.'

'The difficult part is to take out the men on the mountain,' Stan continued. 'They can shoot down on us, whereas it's more tricky for them if they shoot standing up level with us on the ground. The good news is, I imagine they won't have monster sniper rifles. There's no degree of certainty if they are using Kalashnikovs. Think you can handle that, Johnny?'

'No problem,' I said. 'If I've got a target, I can take it out.'

'I'll put you in the central shooting position,' Stan said. 'Bull to the right and me on the left. I've laid out two rows of shooting positions, one for attack and one for defence. The shooting positions are made from sandbags. Underneath each sandbag, I've put a spare clip of bullets and a bottle of water.'

'Red?' I said. 'What's it looking like from your side? Can you pull it off?'

'I've done a dry one, which worked, but I can't guarantee it. Who knows the reaction at dawn tomorrow?'

'Then it's as good as we can hope for,' I said. 'We go with it.'

'We can expect we will be outnumbered at least six to one,' Bull said, 'but I'll take those odds. They've never been in a fight before. They will panic at the slightest turn of misfortune, and get careless if they sense victory. Like all of Johnny's plans, it will rely on a slice of luck, but I'd place my money on us. And just let no one disagree.'

'Dawn is at five o'clock,' I said. 'We set off whenever we are ready after dinner. Put your hands on the table.'

Left hands were placed on the table five times high. We had a green light. All systems go.

CHAPTER FIFTEEN

In the dark a wild dog gave a ghostly howl that chilled me to the bone. It was the sound of my long-time enemy — Death. I took a sip of water from the bottle under the sandbag, and I felt the spare ammunition. It was comforting.

An hour before dawn, I saw the lights from two vehicles draw up on the other side of the fence, one a jeep, the other a truck. Men came out of each — more than twenty was my guess. A little less than I expected, but it was hard to tell in the pre-dawn gloom. I kept a special eye on the jeep: the leaders would be travelling in that, rather than crammed into the truck.

Time to test the sniper rifle.

I looked through the telescopic sight for more detail. The man who stepped out of the passenger seat of the jeep was short and fat. I put him down on both counts as the man in charge. I took aim, held my breath and pressed the trigger.

A spark of light from the sniper rifle and the bullet hit him in the neck. He rocked back from the force and fell to the ground, unmoving.

First blood to us.

Three men ran to the shelter of the mountain. The rest dived for cover. I changed my aim to the three running up the mountain and took one out before they knew what was happening. The other two looked behind and saw their fallen comrade. That pause gave me time to take out another. The third man ducked behind a boulder and I lost him. I wasn't worried. He would give his position away the moment he put up his head up to shoot.

Bull, behind and on my right, let off a blast from his assault rifle. The enemy were still prostrate on the ground, unsure what to do. Stan, behind and on the left, fired. We needed them to be closer.

For a while, nothing moved and no shots were fired. Heartened by that, the main body of the enemy crawled forward to the fence. Then they started to fire on us. Their bullets harmlessly hit the sandbags. Stan had done well on our defences. Time was on our side.

Bull let out a piercing scream, as if hit. All part of the plan. There was a cheer from the opposing force, and all of them crawled to the fence.

To win the battle — to win the war — we had to take out every last one of the enemy. We couldn't do that while they were all lying down. We set off three rounds of bullets and waited.

One of the men started work on the electric fence wires with a pair of insulated bolt cutters. He had backup from a covering burst from behind him. He was an easy target for the sniper rifle. I fired and hit him in the shoulder.

First bad shot of the night.

The man ran to the cover of the truck and was replaced by another. The insulated bolt cutters started to make progress. Bull waited till the man made headway on the fence and let off a burst from the Kalashnikov and shot him down.

He, in turn, was replaced by another, who started to pull back the section of fence that had been cut. The men now passed through to our side of the fence. They started shooting out of sheer bravado. Nothing came close to us.

Now came the tricky bit. Well, the first of two tricky bits, actually. We would expose ourselves during the manoeuvre, but reckoned we would run and jink faster than they could shoot as they worked out what was happening.

'Retreat!' I shouted.

We got up and ran back to the other set of firing positions. We threw ourselves down and took the aim that was part of the plan. We shot short as if we were outside the range of their positions. The enemy grew more confident.

Now was the second tricky bit.

'Now!' I shouted. 'Come on, Red. Do your stuff.'

There was movement in the trees. Red appeared with hands held high and fingers in the position he had used previously. He was running. Behind him came the herd of elephants.

Perhaps surprisingly, given their bulk, elephants can run fast.

The enemy just stared, unable to work out what was happening.

At the last moment, Red ran sideways and leaped to the ground. The elephants carried on. Straight to the enemy.

Not a soul was left alive after the elephants' heavy feet had trampled over the bulky bodies.

We'd done it. We had pulled off the audacious plan. We let out the deep breath that we had been holding.

It was poetic justice. It was irony. The poachers killed by their prey. The elephants would have peace from now on.

We stood and came together, walking to inspect the crumpled bodies. We checked them and put a couple out of their misery.

It was all over.

We shook hands and congratulated each other.

'At last one of your plans worked, Johnny,' said Bull.

'I'll remind you of this day whenever you doubt me,' I said.

'I'm sure you'd do that many times in the future whether I doubt you or not,' he said. 'You are going to be insufferable.'

Stan put his arms around Red in a bear hug. 'Wonderful. Who would have believed it? To show my appreciation, I'll let you drive me back to the base camp. No other praise could reach those heights.'

'God, I love you, Red,' I said. 'I'll never rebuke you when you talk of Comanches ever again.'

'Manitou is a great god to have on your side,' Red said. 'Plus the experience of mesmerising buffalo in the old days. They say only some have that gift. I have been lucky.'

'I suppose Munroe will have to be told,' I said, 'but I'd like to leave that for a little while. My priority is an ice-cold beer and a big shot of vodka. The animals can eat their fill of the bodies until then.'

The wild dog howled again. It wasn't so ghostly this time. Nothing could chill me now.

I was on the crest of a wave. We had won. We could go home. What a lovely moment.

We collected up our weapons and spare ammunition and got into the jeeps — Red and Stan in one, me and Bull in the other, and motored down the track to the base camp. We got out and walked with our heads held high.

'Drop your weapons!'

It was uttered by a Chinese man pressing a revolver against Ibo's head.

Hell! That's what you get when you have too much pride. It's called hubris — what you get when you think yourself better than the gods. It's followed by Nemesis — the goddess of retribution.

We laid down our arms.

CHAPTER SIXTEEN

There were ten men in the camp, standing in a circle around the guests. For now, their weapons were pointed at the four of us. If it wasn't for the presence of the guests, I was certain that we could have triumphed over them, but if we tried now, Ibo would be dead and the guests would follow.

What a stupid mistake to make, I reprimanded myself. That's why there were fewer men opposing us at the fence than I had expected. Had it all been for nothing? They'd laid a trap for us, and we'd fallen right into it.

I saw Pieter on the ground, a trickle of blood from his head forming a pool on the earth. I didn't know how hurt he was, but at least the blood was only a trickle.

Jesse was standing at the front of one of the rows of guests. He looked old. That's what fear does to you. There were other things, too, and I didn't want to think about them. Joni had become separated from him. She was standing next to Penelope.

The Chinese man said something to one of his men, and he gathered up our weapons and carried them inside the office. They should have searched us. We still had our knives. Some hope, then. We just needed an opportunity to make them regret it.

'Here's the deal,' said the Chinese man. 'I could kill you all now, but I won't. You are men who almost certainly know other mercenaries. If I kill you, then maybe others will come to seek vengeance. I will let you go. Think yourself fortunate. In a moment, you will pack your things. We will then tie you up, put you in a jeep and take you to the airport. Then you will be free. However, we will take the boy and two women as hostages, in case you think of returning. Those two.' He pointed at Joni and Penelope — what a mistake that was. She could rob them of the will to live.

Two men from the poachers' gang pulled Penelope and Joni out.

'Get your filthy hands off my Joni,' Jesse said. He took out the gun I had given him, disobeying the condition that there must be no heroics. He pointed it at the Chinese man. 'Touch her again and I will kill you.'

Three bullets thumped into him and he fell to the floor. Quickly, I went to him — the poachers didn't stop me — and I rolled him over to examine the damage. The wounds looked bad. So close to his heart that I thought it would be touch and go for him. His eyes were blinking.

'Don't you die on me, old man,' I said. 'I forbid it. Your time is yet to come. Keep your eyes open. Don't go to sleep. Don't die on me,' I repeated. I slapped his face. 'If you give in, who will I share a sundowner with?'

I slapped him again, and his eyes flickered back at me.

'This man needs an ambulance.' I picked up the gun. 'Let us call one, or I will shoot you dead. I am quicker than him and more accurate. I can take you out before you press that trigger. Put a clip of ammunition on the floor.'

One of his men did so and I fired, sending it skittering away. I shot again, and caught it again. One more bullet hitting it, and I had made my point. 'Kill me and I take you down with me.'

'Very well,' the leader said. 'Make the call and put the gun down.'

'Stan,' I said. 'Call an ambulance.'

When he had been successful, I placed the gun on the floor to show my agreement to anything he asked.

One of his men went to scoop it up.

'No,' I said. 'This is what he would have wanted.'

I placed the gun in Jesse's hand and stood up. It's how he wanted to die, he had said: with a gun in his hand. I was still hoping it wouldn't come to that.

Joni was screaming and being held back by her guard. She wanted to come to Jesse and comfort him. To remember the life they had had before. Hold his hand. Take him in her arms.

'Tie them up,' said the Chinese man. 'Take them away.'

Bull looked across at me.

I shook my head. *Now is not the time.*

They left Pieter on the floor, his head still bleeding. If he could hold on, he and Jesse could go together in the ambulance. Maybe, just maybe, they would live.

They tied our hands behind our backs and manhandled us into a jeep — Stan in the front seat and the rest of us crammed in a space designed for two.

'Don't suppose you have anything Comanche that would be a way out of this mess,' I said to Red.

'A Comanche would not have got himself in this mess in the first place,' he replied.

'Hardly helpful,' I said, 'but I'll remind myself of that next time.'

With hands tied behind our backs, we couldn't reach our knives. But, and it was a big but, we could reach one another's.

'Time to cosy up,' said Bull. 'Who goes first?'

'I do you first, I said, 'then it's freedom time.'

'Now would be a good time for a riveting conversation, Stan,' I said.

'What's your name?' he asked the driver. 'We might as well be friendly.'

I twisted round in the seat so that I could rest my hand on his leg. I opened the flap of the pocket and slid out his knife. Bull now twisted round to the left and I twisted to the right. Hell of a lot of twisting involved. Now was the tricky part. I couldn't see his ropes and had to work blind. I used the serrated edge of the commando knife and started to saw, hoping I didn't cut his hands.

'Yell, if it starts to hurt,' I said.

'Just do it,' Bull said. 'What's a slashed wrist got to do with it?'

I continued to saw and felt the bonds come loose.

'Just a little task to do, and I'll repay you,' Bull said.

He took the knife and placed it along the guard's neck.

'Listen carefully,' he said to the driver. 'I'll slash your throat right now if you don't do what I say. Pull over and stop the car. Do it slowly. I wouldn't like to slit your throat by accident. That would be much less fun. Now.'

The driver slowed down and came to a halt on the side of the road. He was sweating profusely and shaking.

Bull slit my bonds and then Red's. Stan eased himself from his front seat, and I climbed out and freed him.

'Well, Stan,' I said, 'you're the tactician. What do we do to this man?'

'We could cut his fingers off so that he can't use his phone,' Stan said.

The driver started crying. 'No! I'll do whatever you want — Take my phone. I won't scream or anything.'

'Search him,' I said.

Bull patted him down and found a handgun — not much, but it might do for a start. I slid out the clip and checked: it was full of bullets. We also took his phone and threw it away.

'Get out,' Stan said. 'Red, you drive. Find us a deserted spot.'

Stan pushed the driver between me and Bull.

'Be a good boy,' Bull said, 'and I might not kill you. Although I must admit that I'm feeling a little grumpy. Edgy, too. I'll try not to shoot you by mistake, but you'll understand if I do, I hope.'

Red turned the jeep around and we headed back in the direction of the camp. A couple of miles later, there was a sign for a mine. Red pulled off the road and on to a track.

In the distance, there was a giant digger. Red headed for it. He stopped the jeep. 'This should do.'

We all got out and made a length of rope by tying together what was left of our bonds. We tied the driver's hands behind his back and his ankles together. We frisked him again, making sure he was clean. Better safe than sorry. Then it was a simple job for Bull to lift up the driver and put him in the bucket of the digger, then tuck him down so he was out of sight.

'I suppose no one wants it to end here,' I said. 'Am I right that everyone wants to head back and redeem ourselves? Fulfil the promise. Captives to rescue, too. Are we all agreed?'

Everyone nodded.

'Time to burn some rubber,' I said to Red.

'When isn't it?' He floored the accelerator.

CHAPTER SEVENTEEN

We parked the jeep a mile away from the camp and jogged the rest of the way. We had one handgun and four commando knives. Not a lot, but we had God on our side — isn't that what they always say? Manitou as well. Plus the fact that we were sneaky. Sneaky always counts for a lot.

We let ourselves in, not making a sound. We would take up a formation when we were close to the interior of the camp. There was no one on guard at the entry. All those men and they couldn't spare one to patrol the gate? Ridiculous.

There was no talking between us, just hand signals brought about by experience. We spread out. I pointed Bull to my right, Stan to the left and Red following on behind me in the centre. I had our lone handgun — me firing it would be the signal to break from cover and take the camp. Jesse was not in sight. Hopefully he was off to the hospital with some life still in him. Pieter was still lying on the ground, the trickle of blood dried up.

We took out knives and crept closer. I paused just outside the centre of the camp and peeked around to see what was happening. There were four guards. Two at the stockade where the guests had been shepherded, I guessed — hopefully with Ibo, Joni and Penelope among them. Another guard was outside the office and one was at the kitchen, nonchalantly eating a sandwich.

The one outside the office was my target. That was where the guns were kept. It was a sideways target for me rather than full width, but I had had worse in the past.

Here we go.

I fired and all hell was let loose: we shouted so loud it could burst your eardrums. The man outside the office fell forward. There was a lot of blood from his neck where my bullet had landed.

Stan appeared behind the man at the kitchen and slit his throat. Red grabbed his shotgun from the office and went to the stockade. I heard two booms from the shotgun and made that the full quota of guards.

We let the guests and the three rangers out of the stockade and took them to the tables and chairs. Red found a couple of bottles of brandy and poured large glasses for everyone. No one declined.

We had hoped that by a slim chance, the captives would be among them, but that wouldn't suit any purpose. Munty was there, in floods of tears, her mind focused on Ibo and what might be happening to him.

If there was any time for vodka, it was now. Stan did the honours. One small glass each, for this would not be the end of things. We would need a cool head for what was to come.

'Our first priority is to look after the guests,' I said, 'but that, we can leave to the rangers. Stan, get Ranu organising transport to the airport. Meanwhile, we need to put a plan in action. I'll make the necessary arrangements, and then we storm the base and free Ibo, Joni and Penelope. That's where they must be.'

'We could leave it all to Munroe to sort out,' said Stan.

'And how long will that take?' I said. 'What might they do to the captives in that time? It's down to us to sort out.'

'You left out the other reason,' said Bull. 'Ain't no personal satisfaction in it if we leave it all to Munroe. We need to get back at them. Show the Chinese who is boss, and that they don't mess with us. No one takes my gun and tells me to ride on.'

'Right,' I said. 'Action.'

We downed the vodka and prepared to go. I made an impromptu speech to the guests to pack and be ready to leave. There was no danger anymore. They could all sigh and let out the breath they were holding. They could go home and bask in the limelight that freedom would give them. It was, in some ways, the adventure they all had hoped for. Different, but still the trip of a lifetime. I finished with a plea not to make any phone calls till they were at the airport, so as not to endanger the lives of the captives.

Speech over, now came the hard part. We loaded up the weapons. That's when Pieter rolled over and started to come round.

'What the hell happened?'

'What happened is you are the luckiest sonofabitch in the world,' I said. 'You missed the fun, but there's more to come. Grab your weapons and be ready for the battle. Fill in your part of the story.'

'They came from both sides — entry and top fence,' he said. 'I fired off some bullets and took a couple down, then someone slugged me from behind. I must have passed out. That's all I remember.'

'We'll fill you in when we're on our way to the Chinese base. All you need to know at the moment is that the poachers are holding Ibo, Joni and Penelope. We're going to set them free.'

'Did I miss vodka?' He looked at the empty glasses on the table. 'Time to catch up.'

He lifted the bottle to his lips and took a swig. 'Everything seems better after vodka.'

'That's what I've been telling you all these years,' said Stan.

'Will it help me be a hero?' Pieter said.

'Time will tell,' I said.

* * *

The fire engine arrived ten minutes later. If you're going to hire a few men, it makes sense that the transport comes with them. There were four firefighters aboard, all looking like they could storm a castle with their bare hands. They had that toned appearance of men and women who worked out and were forever handling heavy equipment. There was space inside for a dozen occupants, and we five got on board.

Stan gave instructions as to where we were going and, being in charge of our funds, counted out some bills and paid them the fee in advance. I explained that their role would be suppression rather than attacking, and that hoses would be their main weapon.

They turned on the sirens and flashing lights about a mile from the house, so as to build authenticity that an emergency was taking place, and pulled up at the gates. There were two men on guard and they swung the gates open for us. Neither of the guards questioned us — who was going to turn away a fire engine? Madness, surely.

As we approached the house, three men, fully armed, greeted us. For some reason, they doubted us. Maybe because there was no smoke, or maybe they were just edgy, whatever — but now was the time to attack.

We jumped from the fire engine. The hoses were reeled out, and the five of us ran towards the building. We ran as far as we could outside the danger zone and dived to the ground before the men opened fire.

We started shooting and the men took cover behind the pillars at the entrance. It had all of the signs of a stalemate.

We took our positions. Bull ran to the left, Stan to the right and Red coming to join me in the middle. We were widening our attack area and coming at them in a pincer movement. I signalled to the firefighters to start the deluge.

The power of the hose knocked the men down and left the field of fire to us. We started shooting. The men were overwhelmed and fell to the floor, all life departed. *Dead* would be a shorter description, but you have to allow poetic licence sometimes.

Bull ran to the door. It was locked, but he used the spare set of keys he had obtained — by fair means or foul — from the estate agent. He swung the door open and we joined him. In a classic defence movement, we entered, Bull first and then I overlapped him, and vice versa until we had the downstairs under control.

At the back of the corridor was a kitchen, where a fat Chinese man was trying to squeeze through an impossibly small window. I waved Stan, Red and Pieter to check out upstairs and turned my attention to the trainee escapologist.

'Never heard about quarts and pint pots? Drop any weapons you have and put your hands up in the air. Bull, frisk him.'

He wasn't armed and, I suspected, wouldn't know one end of a gun from the other.

Stan, Pieter and Red reappeared and shook their heads. No joy upstairs, it seemed.

'What's your name?'

'Why does that matter?'

'I like to keep count of those I kill,' I said. 'I keep a record in a leather-bound notebook. I like to have names to put down rather than just "Chinese man".'

'Ding,' he said.

'Where are they, Ding?' I said. 'Where are you hiding them?'

'They're not here.'

'Then where are they?' I persevered. 'If you don't tell me, I'm going to set Bull on you. He'll probably begin by putting two bullets through your knees and then start cutting off your fingers one by one while you're slumped on the floor. Show him your knife, Bull.'

Bull took out his commando knife and tapped the blade against the palm of his hand.

Ding shivered. Right response. There's something about a serrated edge that makes a knife more threatening — it's the prospect of sawing to come, I reckon.

'They've moved on.'

'To where?' I said.

'To the boss's house,' the man said.

Then it all became clear. The knowledge the poachers had of the movements and routines of the reserve. Maybe the safari business wasn't profitable on its own. Or maybe it was greed. Pure greed. Gamekeeper turned poacher. A hundred grand a pair of tusks was irresistible. Maybe Van Lloyd wouldn't slaughter the whole herd. Not all at once, at least. He needed a few to satisfy the guests' longings to see elephants as part of their safari.

'Tell me all,' I said to Ding. 'What's going on?'

'The boss hired us to get some ivory. Paid us a commission. I arranged for the local labour. I'm just a middleman taking the ivory to China. No more than a courier, really.'

'And did being a middleman extend to trying to kill us?'

'I didn't like doing it,' he said, as if that made it all right. 'Couldn't see any alternative. I thought you'd give up and move on. Why didn't you do that?'

'Because we had made a promise, and promises need to be honoured, otherwise what's the point?' I said. 'How many times do I have to say it to people? We're only wasting valuable time. Find something to tie him up, Stan, and let's get moving.'

I turned back to the firefighters and told them that we needed a rerun. Another castle to storm.

Stan had found a length of rope in the garage and tied up the Chinese man and put him at the back of the house where he wouldn't be seen.

We moved the bodies of the guards to join him. Then we got in the fire engine.

Onward and upward.

* * *

The guards weren't so compliant at Van Lloyd's house. They said there were no signs of a fire and refused to open the gates.

I looked at a firefighter. 'Any ideas?'

'Do you know how heavy one of these fire engines is?'

'No,' I said, hoping that this would be relevant in some way.

'Neither do I,' he said, 'but it's too much for these gates.'

The driver turned the fire engine around and backed it up to the gates so that it was touching. Then he simply let out the clutch and pushed. The gates stood no chance.

'Told you,' the firefighter said. 'Same procedure?'

'Yep. You man the hoses and we'll do the shooting.'

There were three guards on duty outside the house. They started shooting as soon as we jumped from the fire engine. We ran forward and then dived to the ground, firing as we did so.

There wasn't much of a target for us to aim at. Then we had a stroke of luck and an act of bravery.

One of the men lobbed a hand grenade at us. It landed barely ten yards away and rolled closer.

'I got it!' Pieter leaped forward, picked up the grenade and in one movement threw it back at them.

They were still firing, and Pieter went down.

The grenade exploded and took out the three men on guard.

The door opened. Van Lloyd emerged with a gun to Joni's head. Two further men came out, each holding guns on Penelope and Ibo.

'I should have killed you earlier,' he said. 'It was a mistake letting you go from the camp, but who but a fool would come back?'

'A man of honour,' I said.

'You can turn around now,' he said, 'or we can shoot you down. You'll never be able to shoot us before we kill our hostages.'

We laid our assault rifles on the ground and took the Hi-Powers out of the holsters.

'Do you reckon you can beat us?' I said. 'You're facing the best five shots in the land, if not in the universe, actually.

My advice would be to let our people go and hand yourself over to Munroe.'

He'd probably get a life sentence in some flea-ridden, rat-infested cell, but at least he'd be alive. If you could call it life.

'Put your guns down,' I said.

I looked across at Bull on my left.

He nodded.

I checked with Stan on my right.

He nodded.

'We fire on the count of three. One.'

We fired. Always got them, the count-of-three trick. We shot them in between their eyes and they fell to the ground.

Ibo, Penelope and Joni were free, never in any danger from our shots.

I went across to Pieter and an idea came to me. Two in one day is not bad.

I bent down and spoke. 'You're dead, Pieter. You have fought your last battle. Understand? It was good to know you. Maybe things will get better now.' I shouted, 'Someone get something to cover him up! He goes with dignity.'

I bade the firefighters goodbye and asked them loudly to take Pieter to the morgue.

'Stan, see you if you can find some keys to the jeeps,' I said. 'It's time to head back and finish that bottle of vodka.'

Red went with Stan to the back of the house, and pretty soon two jeeps pulled up in front of us. Red gunned the engine on one of them, impatient to get to the rest of the vodka.

Penelope ran up to me and clung to me. She was sobbing and shaking. I held her close, and the crying ebbed away.

'Pieter?' she said. 'What's happened to Pieter?'

'I'm afraid that Pieter didn't make it,' I said, 'but he died a hero's death.'

'Can I see him?'

'He's on his way to the morgue,' I said, 'but you wouldn't have recognised him. A grenade is a brutal weapon. It was the

156

way he would have wanted to go. I'm sure his dying thoughts would have been love for you.'

Joni came to join us. 'What's happened to Jesse? Is he OK?'

'As far as I know,' I said, 'he's in hospital. We'll check when we get back to base camp. If he's up to having a visitor, I'll drive you there. First, we need some respite, to breathe for a while. It's been a busy day. We need to take stock and work out what needs to happen, now you're all safe.'

I looked at Bull. Ibo was wrapped in his arms. Ibo had done well to keep calm when the shots were ringing out. He would have learned a lot today about not giving up hope.

Goes for all of us, I suppose. Never too old to learn.

CHAPTER EIGHTEEN

Jesse was stable — that was the outcome of our calls to the hospital. I breathed a sigh of relief and told Joni I would drive her there after one thing I needed to do. Munroe.

When he arrived, Munroe wasn't a happy bunny. 'I am getting reports of three incidents, gunshots and a bomb,' he said. 'Like to fill me in?'

'It wasn't a bomb,' I said. 'It was a hand grenade.'

'That would make it all right, then?'

'Technically, makes little difference, I suppose,' I said, 'but it's good to get the facts straight.'

'Something as a police officer with twenty-five years' experience, I wouldn't know about, right? So tell me these facts.'

'Where to begin?'

'It's a cliché,' he said, 'but the beginning is usually best.'

'It all started with a fight at the west fence,' I said. 'We left the bodies of around twenty men for the hyenas. If you go there in the morning, you should find enough remains to corroborate that part of the story.'

'Only twenty bodies,' Munroe said. 'Slow day, was it?'

'We made it up later,' I said. 'The battle was supposed to be the end of everything — if we won, the poachers would give up, if we lost, we'd be dead men.'

'So I take it you won,' he said, 'seeing as there are twenty bodies and you're here to tell the tale.'

'It was a Pyrrhic victory,' I said. 'We won the battle but lost the war. Before we had a chance to celebrate, the poachers had taken the camp here. The attack on the western fence was really a diversion. They took away three hostages and let us go. If we didn't give in, the hostages would be killed.'

'Let's just get things straight,' Munroe said. 'They let you go. I think I see where this is going. You were stubborn, I take it.'

'I prefer to call it single-minded.'

'Let's not get into semantics. What next?'

'We came back and retook the camp. You'll find four dead men spread around. Didn't have any time to give them a decent burial.'

'So, we're up to twenty-four bodies?' he said. 'I have a sinking feeling I know what comes next. Carry on.'

'We thought the poachers would have taken the hostages back to the house of a Chinese man called Ding. Stormed the place.'

'Was that where the fire engine came into play?'

'Ah, the fire engine,' I said. 'You know about that.'

'Seemed like a lot of calls from local residents worried about their safety,' he said. 'You wouldn't know anything about that. Sirens and flashing lights are a bit hard to ignore.'

'We thought it best to play "safe not sorry",' I said. 'Hard to know whether to allow for a fire to break out in any confusion. Purely precautionary.'

'How many this time?' he asked.

'Just three,' I said, 'although there was a lot of action and I might have lost count.'

'Now we're up to twenty-seven,' Munroe said. 'Ish.'

'The hostages weren't there,' I continued. 'Ding told us that Van Lloyd was behind everything. The lust for ivory was too great to resist. Van Lloyd's place was where the grenade came into play. The guards threw it at us and Pieter threw it back. I knew he'd come right in the end.'

'How many were killed by the grenade?'

'Three.'

'Thirty, am I right?'

'Exactly. But that wasn't the end of it.'

'I'm sure not,' he said. 'Anything is plausible for you.'

'Van Lloyd and two men came out of the house with guns to the heads of the three hostages.'

'Would have been a tricky situation,' he said. 'I dread to ask, but what happened next?'

'We shot them between their eyes.'

'Clarification, please,' he said. 'The men have got guns pressed up against the heads of the hostages and you shot them between their eyes? Wouldn't that have been a teeny bit risky? What if you had missed?'

'There was never any doubt. We're crack shots. We've been practising for years, plus a lot of battles fought around the world for real.'

'Final tally?'

'Another three,' I said. 'I make that thirty-three. Now it is over, and soon we can go home. Another couple of tasks to go and we're there.'

'And your freelance crime wave stops,' Munroe said, 'and I can get back to the simple life. What do you suggest I do first to dredge this mire out of existence?'

'Get yourself a big truck to take away the bodies,' I said. 'Then search Van Lloyd's house. You're sure to find some ivory there. Tie it up with a pretty ribbon.'

'I'll send some uniformed officers to take statements, although I know they'll be scratching their heads at what you say. This is not the Wild West. There is no place for vigilantes around here.'

'Not anymore, that is.'

'Are you always like this?' he said. 'Are you always a magnet for corpses?'

'Trouble seems to follow me around,' I said. 'Sometimes gets ahead of me, too, if I'm honest. Meanwhile, on to practicalities. What will happen to the reserve, now that Van Lloyd is dead?'

'It will go up for sale.'

'Any likely takers?'

'Maybe the reserve on the northern boundary will buy it and turn it into one big reserve. That's the most feasible possibility. Or maybe there's someone out there with pots of money, looking for something good for it. Who knows? It's a wacky world — you're proof of that.'

'Can the animals survive with no one looking over them?'

'There's plenty of food out there,' he said. 'Natural grazing for the plant feeders and prey for the predators. They'll be all right unless there's some sort of emergency, when you'd need people to spot something wrong and call in a vet, for example.'

'What about poachers?' I said. 'Will they have a free run if no one's on patrol?'

'I doubt anyone would risk it. This story will get out and the poachers will go somewhere else. The safaris are a different matter. I've never been happy with all this camping out. The guests are so vulnerable outside of their trucks. One guest death and the whole business model collapses. Things would have to be very different. If a buyer is found, I don't think there should be any effects on the people here. Guests still have to eat and drink and see the wildlife. Doesn't have to be anything too ambitious.'

'So we're in the clear then?' I asked. 'You're not going to put us in chokey?'

'Frankly, I'll be glad to see you go, when I have my working hat on. I hate to think about how much paperwork you've generated.'

'And with your personal hat on?' I said.

'You're a breath of fresh air. You certainly livened the place up.'

'Are we chums?' I said.

'I don't know if I would go that far,' he said, 'even if I knew what you meant by "chums". Something more than acquaintances, though. I'll send you a Christmas card, if that clarifies matters. Now, off you go to the hospital and let me get on with doing my job.'

I shook his hand and it felt warm and he lingered over it. I'd go for 'chums' after all.

* * *

By the time Joni and I set off for the hospital, it was dark and windy. The open-top jeep was not the best vehicle to be travelling in under those conditions. I set the heating on the highest I could get, but it was still cold — the nights came quickly here and the temperature dropped rapidly due to the cloudless skies during the day.

'How were you treated by the poachers?' I said.

'The conditions were fine,' Joni said. 'They gave us food and water, but there was always an ever-present threat. It hung on us like a dark cloud. There was an armed guard on us at all times, and we didn't know what they would do. The native guards were edgy — they wanted vengeance for the friends that had been killed — and it felt as though a storm could erupt at any moment. Van Lloyd only thought of the money and our worth as hostages. I got the impression that he felt it was a done deal, that you would take the safe route and give in. I thought that, too. I didn't know you well enough, did I? Jesse told me that you had a code, and that dictated your actions. It was the force that drove you on.'

'Without the code,' I said, 'we'd just be mercenaries who cared only for the money. Nothing better than homicidal killers who would change sides with a sufficient bribe. I've met a lot of those over the years and they were not nice people. Brutal killers, rapists, torturers — people who would stop at nothing if it would earn them a buck and give them the opportunity to satisfy their sadistic tendencies. We five gravitated together because we were kindred spirits. We looked for a cause we believed in. One that might keep our consciences clean.'

'Shame that it all turned out so badly,' Joni said. 'I was enjoying the whole experience of the safari. Not just viewing the animals from a distance, but getting up close to know them deeply, like you were seeing the world through their eyes. The overnight camps gave me a thrill. That sense of danger. Jesse thought the same. He hasn't had so much fun in years. He's been a changed man here, and you're part of that. He said he always felt safe when you were around. I do so hope he will be all right.'

'They are letting us see him,' I said. 'That must be a good sign.'

She went quiet. 'You gave him the gun, didn't you? You gave him the chance to be a hero. To die with a gun in his hand, just like he wanted. To join those brave friends he'd lost in Vietnam.'

'I never thought he would have cause to use it, but who could predict what happened today?'

'What about your friend Pieter?' she said. 'What transpired there?'

'I would rather not talk about that,' I said.

'I understand. There will be a time when the memories become less fresh and can be absorbed in the cold light of day.'

'Something like that,' I said. 'To change the subject, tell me about Ibo.'

'He was always calm,' she said. 'He had an inner confidence that Bull would come and rescue him. Penelope and I drew strength from him. If you had to choose someone with whom to be a hostage, then it would be Ibo.'

'And Penelope?'

'She treats him so badly,' Joni said. 'It's embarrassing. Like it was the height of Apartheid here. Like he was a third-class citizen and counted for nothing.'

'I have a plan for that,' I said. 'Leave it with me.'

'I suppose we should cut her some slack now that she has seen Pieter killed in such a dramatic fashion. I have sympathy for her on that. Who wouldn't? It will take her a while to get over that. I know how I will feel when Jesse passes.'

'Let's hope we have a while before that.'

We pulled into the hospital car park, which was eerily quiet, as by now it was the early hours of the morning. We checked in with the lone receptionist, who told us the ward Jesse was in and to follow blue on the colour-coded flooring. We passed a coffee shop — still open for those who needed a caffeine hit to get them through the night — and I thought it might be wise to have a double espresso after seeing Jesse, to help keep me awake during the drive back.

The main lights on the ward were off and a soft blue radiance glowed from the ceiling to help patients go to sleep and nurses to find their way around. There was a nurses' station, where two women in blue uniforms sat going through some notes on clipboards. One of them took us to where Jesse was propped up with no signs of sleep. Nearby, a man was snoring heavily, the regular noise akin to the dripping tap torture once employed by the Chinese to break down the will of the prisoners. The nurse told us that we could only stay fifteen minutes, as Jesse was still weak. But he was alive — that was the important thing.

He smiled at us, a good sign.

Joni perched on the bed and I sat in the well-padded armchair where the patient could rest during the day, if they were up to it.

Joni took hold of Jesse's hand. 'You're alive,' she said. 'God be praised.'

'But not totally in one piece, so they tell me,' said Jesse. 'They say I am lucky to be alive, that it was touch and go. The bullets hit me in the shoulder, rather than my heart, and passed straight through. They didn't have to dig them out, for which I'm thankful. They've patched me up and given me some blood to top up how much I lost, plus a truckload of painkillers. I can go home in a couple of days if I'm a good boy. I'm supposed to rest, but that seems unnecessary given my age and general health — the big C and such. I've been doing that for too long. I certainly don't want to spend my days in hospital with a man who snores at sixty decibels.'

'I thought I told you not to be a hero, old man,' I said.

'Then you shouldn't have given me the gun.'

'There is that, I suppose, now you've brought it up. What did you think you were doing?'

'Protecting my Joni,' he said. 'No one harms my Joni if I'm around. I'd fight to the death for her.'

'I understand. Do you not know what transpired since you were carted off here? Don't you wonder how Joni is here sitting on your bed?'

'Oh, I know that,' he said. 'You would free her at some stage, I knew, as simple as that. She wasn't in any danger with you around. How many men did you have to kill?'

'It's a moot point,' I said. 'I've been through it with Captain Munroe. But it was always about the ivory. The desire for it and the wealth that it brings. A magical material. You didn't meet him, but the man behind it was a guy called Van Lloyd. He owned the safari business and wanted some money on the side. He was behind the poaching and had a channel through to the Chinese dealers, selling it on for decoration and some quack medicine.'

'So what did you do with him?'

'We killed him, of course,' I said. 'Well, me, I suppose. Bull took the guard on the left, and Stan the one on the right.'

'You wouldn't believe it,' said Joni. 'Van Lloyd and his guards had the three of us as human shields. The shooting from Johnny and his friends was the most accurate you would ever see. Three shots, all between the eyes. And you know what? I never felt in danger at any time. This was a story that would always have a happy ending.'

'So what will happen to the reserve,' Jesse said, 'now that this Van Lloyd guy is dead?'

'They will try to sell it off. I don't know what the finances are like — whether the safari business is a growing concern, but there are opportunities, I would think.'

'I could be interested,' Jesse said. 'I'll give you the name of one of our financial people. Get him some numbers. Got a pen, Joni?'

She dug in her bag and produced a small leather note-book and a Montblanc pen. That's style. Jesse wrote down a number, tore off the page and gave it to me.

'Are you serious?' I said. 'This is a wildlife reserve and a safari business. It's like nothing I've ever heard of. I don't know the rules that govern it. It's a shot in the dark.'

'And you would know about that,' he said.

'That's different,' I said. 'I can hit a target blindfold, if Bull is around. I know the game and what you have to do to win it.'

'Look at it this way,' he said. 'The safaris are too cheap. Give it a touch of luxury and you could double the price. I'd build a big lodge with all the facilities. Keep the safari close and personal, though. Twenty guests would be fine — make it too big, and the atmosphere goes. Have just the one night at a camp for the total experience.'

'But why?' I said. 'Why would you do that?'

'For the excitement. I've only a couple of years tops to live, why not go out with a bang? Do something left field for a change. I'd buy it as a toy. Something to play with. What better way to go?'

'Better than with a gun in your hand?'

'That would still be an alternative.'

'Are you feeling OK?' said Joni. 'Have the painkillers affected your brain? Are you thinking straight?'

'It would be an adventure,' Jesse said. 'You can't deny someone an adventure. We've plenty of money, all locked up in companies making widgets or whatever, that make no difference to the world. Let's spend the time we have together in the sun, close up to the animals. We'd make the best room in the lodge for us. Can't you picture it? Bourbon on ice each night as the sun goes down. Let's have some fun, Joni.'

'I know what you're like when you get an idea in your head,' she said. 'Nothing I say will make any difference. Let's just see if you feel the same in the morning.'

'I'll mull it over while I'm here. Maybe get some sleep, too. Do one thing for me, Johnny?'

'Anything you want.'

'Nudge the bed of the man snoring. Wake him up so that I can get some peace.'

Jesse closed his eyes. He looked a tired man, but happy with what fate had handed out. Plenty to dwell on with Joni, on the trip back. He was a man with a dream. We needed more people like that. Having a dream should be a requisite for life. Funny how life can be.

CHAPTER NINETEEN

Ibo woke me up with a cup of tea and a bacon sandwich. It
was eight o'clock and I'd had about three hours sleep. It would
have to do for the time being. Too much to do yet. Dotting
of Is and crossing of Ts.

The guests were awaiting the arrival of a bus to take them
to the airport. There was an atmosphere of relief in the camp.
I wondered just what they would take out of the adventure,
when the dust had settled. It had been exciting, certainly, but
would that generate the five-star reviews that would be needed
if the business was to succeed? They say that any publicity is
good publicity — it increases awareness, for one thing. But
I wasn't so sure, and wondered whether Jesse would feel the
same, in the cold light of day.

I was sitting with my cup of tea and bacon sandwich with
the crew. Everyone looked tired. It's not so much about the
physical effort in a battle that draws on your system, it's the
mental element. The need to be constantly ready to function
at peak level. High alert is fine for a while, but drags you down
when the adrenaline stops flowing.

Ibo seemed to be over his ordeal and Munty was back
to her exuberant self. She said she would cook a special meal

for us all, Joni and Penelope included. I had qualms about that. My mind imagined whether 'special' meant crocodile or some other dubious delicacy shot that morning by the rangers.

I had just finished my breakfast when a couple of the guests came up to me. The man had on dark-blue chinos and a light-blue short-sleeve cotton shirt. The woman was ready for the rigours of travel in a long white dress and silver strappy sandals. Cool and stylish. The man shook my hand and the woman kissed my cheek.

'I suppose we owe you our lives,' the man said.

'No suppose about it,' said the woman. 'I dread to think what might have happened if you hadn't come back. We would all be witnesses and, therefore, at risk. We would have all been silenced by more shooting. "Dead men tell no tales," as the saying goes.'

'Just doing what we do,' said Bull.

'Killing?' the man said.

'Yep,' said Bull. 'Sometimes the planet is better off without some people, and it falls to us to put that matter right. Look at it as if we are around to rid the barrel of the bad apples. The killing bit is just something that has to be done. You get used to it. It's a public service that we do.'

'The Comanches would put the wrongdoer in the desert with only a knife,' said Red. 'The evil one would be expected to do the chivalrous thing and slit his throat. Tough thing, but it has to be done.'

'Shame about Pieter,' the woman said. 'Is that what you would call collateral damage?'

'Without Pieter,' I said, 'we are missing a friend. Penelope will miss him, too. She had a soft spot for him, and would have walked up the aisle with him at some stage in the future. It will hit her hard.'

'I'll take her aside before we leave,' she said. 'Woman to woman. Give her some emotional support. We women understand things in a different way to men. I'll comfort her.'

169

'So there was no military exercise, after all?' said the man. 'I don't know how we would have felt if we had known the truth. Got back on the next plane home, I reckon.'

'And we would have missed all the fun,' said the woman. 'I could have done without the deaths, but no one could deny the excitement we had. What will happen now? Will the safaris continue? We understand the owner died — that's what the eavesdroppers are saying.'

'We might have a buyer,' I said. 'Jesse is interested. He doesn't have all the financials yet, but it's likely, I would say.'

'Such a lovely couple,' the woman said. 'I think they would do a good job here. Jesse's a successful businessman and Joni would make everyone feel the luxury of a safari — that woman's touch. I must admit I felt some qualms about sleeping in the bush, but you were there — you would keep us safe. I needn't have worried.'

'We'd like to give you a gratuity,' the man said. 'A small gesture for looking after us. Would a thousand pounds be acceptable?'

'Very.' I turned to Bull. 'What do you think?'

'Put it in the tips jar for whoever takes over from Pieter to distribute as best as he sees fit,' Bull said. 'I'd like Ibo to get a decent share that could be used for his schooling. 'Reward rather than charity. Go talk to Munty. You will make her very proud of him. He's a good kid and played his part.'

'Joni said you believe in moral values,' the man said. 'That good should always win the battle over evil. That injustice can be put right if we all followed an honourable code. I can see what she means. We will all take away a lot of lessons from our time here. Hell, I'm getting sentimental. Just take our thanks and toast us when you next have a beer.'

He shook our hands, and the woman kissed all our cheeks. She went over to Munty and he brought their suitcases to where the bus would stop.

'Still the same plan?' Red said.

'Precisely,' I said.

'You'll never get away with it,' Stan said. 'Doesn't involve a spreadsheet for one thing.'

'No vodka or pickled gherkins either,' I said. 'Trust me. Trust human behaviour. Trust digging yourself out of a hole.'

'When are you going to put it in action?' said Stan.

'We have to give it a couple of days for the formalities,' I said. 'Get all the details sorted out. It'll come round soon. We're going to have some fun.'

Munty came across to us. She had tears in her eyes.

'Madam came to see me,' she said. 'She said that there could be some money to help with Ibo's schooling. That was your suggestion, wasn't it?

'Ibo needs nurturing,' Bull said. 'I'll be checking up on him in the future. Maybe even come back to see him, from time to time.'

'He would like that,' she said. 'He wants to be like you. You set a good example.'

'Preferably without the killing,' Bull said.

'Without the killing, yes,' said Munty. 'I was going to cook you crocodile tonight, something you don't get to eat very often. A new experience to remember.'

Bonus points for a good guess, Johnny Silver.

'But I think I should let you decide what to eat,' she continued, 'as it's a special day.'

'What would be your choice, guys?' I said.

'Rib-eye steaks,' said Bull.

'Cooked rare over the barbecue,' said Red.

'With chips,' said Stan.

'And with a side salad,' I said.

'Consider it done,' she said. 'It's the least I can do.'

'Got any ketchup?' said Red.

'No,' she said, 'but I'll make you some. Never fear.'

'That's our watchword,' said Red. 'Fear makes you shake and shiver. You can't have that. One shot missed could be the difference between life and death. Focus — that's what you need in a battle.'

'Plus Polish vodka,' Stan said. 'If you are going to die, it's better when the last drink you have is something special.'

'Is it just the six of you tonight?' said Munty. 'The four of you and the two ladies? I'll do something a little more delicate for them. Maybe some fish — see what's freshly caught at the market today. I must go. Ketchup doesn't make itself.'

She took off her apron and got ready to hit the butcher and the fishmonger.

'Well,' said Stan, 'do we grace the ladies with our company or eat on our own?'

'We can't have Joni without Penelope,' I said. 'And we can't let Joni dine with Penelope alone. Joni's got enough to deal with at the moment. Maybe we can dilute Penelope's natural instinct of getting up people's noses with our presence.'

'What's to do today?' said Stan.

'Drinking lots of beer,' I said. 'I have to see the undertakers about the funeral, but will join you after that. See you for lunch. Don't get up to any mischief.'

* * *

The undertakers were a little surprised by my requests, but shrugged and set off to craft a suitable coffin. As always, money was the solution. Why argue when you're getting paid?

I said I wanted the funeral as quickly as possible, and we settled on two days' time. I ordered a simple wreath of red roses — Pieter must have sent a lot of them over the years to various paramours. The four of us would carry the coffin. We could take the weight and felt it was fitting. No help required from them there. No music. The shortest ceremony. I'd give the speech and keep it brief. No fuss.

Penelope grabbed me as soon as I got back. She was sitting on her own at a table. No drink — I didn't know what that meant. Probably that she had just arrived. Was that a good sign or bad? I had not yet made a decision on whether she was more tolerable when drunk or sober. I wondered if

172

Joni had had enough of her company already and was hiding somewhere.

Penelope wanted to know the arrangements for the funeral and to tell me she would fly back as soon as it was over. That didn't suit my plans.

I thought quickly.

'It's going to be a funeral at sea,' I said. 'Pieter always wanted to slip into the Indian Ocean. I don't think the boat trip would suit you unless you're immune to seasickness. Pieter would understand.'

'No,' she said. 'I'll be there. I feel it is my duty to see his coffin slip into the ocean. Only fitting, as I would have been his bride. I would like it to be a tribute to him. I feel he must be honoured.'

'I could give you a copy of my speech and that could be enough for you to save in his memory. It will be a harrowing journey for you.'

'My mind is made up. Now, where's that boy?'

She spotted Ibo standing next to the table where the drinks were laid out.

'Here, boy,' she shouted.

Ibo started to walk towards her.

'Stay there, Ibo,' I said.

'Here, boy!'

'Stay where you are,' I said.

'What's going on?' she said to me.

'You've just been incarcerated with him. In close proximity for many hours. Yet you don't call him by his name. Try again.'

'Here, Ibo,' she said.

'Stay where you are, Ibo.'

'What's the matter now?'

'It's good manners to insert a "please" somewhere in the request.'

'Here, please, Ibo.'

'Stay where you are, Ibo,' I said.

'What now?'

'You didn't say "pretty please".'

'If it will get me a drink, I'll play along. Here, Ibo, pretty please.'

'Perfect,' I said. 'You may move now, Ibo.'

He came to the table. 'How may I serve you?'

'I'd like a dry martini, heavy on the gin,' she said.

'And is there any special gin, madam?'

'I'd like Bombay Sapphire.'

I fought back a smile. I was absolutely certain that they only had one brand of gin — Gordon's — and Ibo had worked out she wouldn't be able to tell the difference.

'And for you, sir?'

'A beer, please, Ibo,' I said. 'Any brand — whatever you've got, as long as it is ice cold.'

'Coming straight up, madam, sir.'

'And I'd like something light with a salad,' she said.

'Of course, madam.' Ibo scurried over to tell Munty the order.

'Wouldn't it be more comfortable to move to a hotel while you're still here?' I said. 'Your own room with a proper bed, hot showers . . . perhaps a touch of luxury in the last of your days in the country.'

'I feel obliged to stay here,' she said.

My God, was there no getting rid of her?

The drinks arrived, with a plate of bobotie. Munty was having fun today. She had her son back and had got some civility from their worst guest ever. What was not to like?

I left Penelope to her supposed light lunch and took my beer over to where the rest of the crew was smiling.

'I told you that you wouldn't get away with it,' said Stan.

'Is there nothing secret here?' I said. 'I've got a few phone calls to make, but it's all under control. All I have to do is hire a boat with a plank, make a few alterations to the basic plan with the undertakers. No problems. I've got it covered.'

Bull grinned at me. 'Oh what a tangled web and such.'

'You're enjoying this, aren't you?' I said.

'I love it when a plan comes together.'

'All plans need to be flexible,' I said.

'And some more flexible than others.'

'Ha, ha. I'm glad you find that funny.'

'It's all relative,' he said.

'That's usually my line,' I said.

'Thought I'd get in before you.'

Joni came along — thankfully — to interrupt the banter. Which was good, because I didn't know what to say next.

'I'm going to see Jesse,' she said.

'I'll drive you,' I said.

'It's fine, I've booked a taxi. I've taken up too much of your time already. Frankly, too, I find the open-top jeep a little nerve-jangling.'

'Could be something that you may have to get used to,' I said.

'Not if I say so. When I spoke to Jesse on the phone earlier, he said to ask you if you made the call to his finance director.'

'I did,' I said, 'but I didn't have much to tell him. I suspect that the information he needs is somewhere in the jumble of the office. I hope I can track it down tomorrow.'

'Jesse would like to attend Pieter's funeral,' she said. 'Thinks we owe everything to you guys and Pieter. It would be a tribute to him.'

'It's going to be a funeral at sea. Do you think Jesse will be up to it? Boat ride and such?'

'He's itching to get back to some semblance of normality. The sea air might do him good.'

And so the guest list grows again. Maybe I should abandon the idea of a small funeral and sell tickets on the nearest high street.

'What time does he leave hospital?' I said.

'As early as possible. He's going stir crazy.'

'The funeral is eleven o'clock,' I said. 'I'll get one of the cars to pick you both up at ten. We could travel back together

175

afterwards. Have a drink together before lunch. There isn't a wake planned, as such, but Munty could rustle up something once she's back here. She and Ibo will be coming along with the rangers. Just a small gathering. Nothing too elaborate.'

'Sounds fitting,' she said. 'Any friends you have will be transient — the guests only here for a week. It can be lonely here, I guess. Something else I might have to get used to.'

'There must be some sort of expat community here. You'd both make lots of friends, I'm sure.' I paused. 'We don't seem to have asked you what you feel about it. Is it something you would be doing under sufferance?'

'Whatever makes Jesse happy,' she said. 'I'd get used to it. It would be a very evocative place to spend your time. Grab each moment while we can. Jesse would love it. A little schmooze with the guests at sundown. Tell them all about Vietnam, whether they're interested or not. Recount this tale, too. Would make a good story,' she said. 'Right. Time to join Lady Penelope, if I must.'

'Another two for the funeral,' Bull said. 'Did it cross your mind to sell tickets in the nearest high street?'

'You know me too well,' I said.

'And I'm still your friend. Who would have guessed it?'

Ibo came over to us. 'My mother would like to know whether you would like some sandwiches.'

'That would be very civilised,' I said, 'and another round of beers, please, Ibo.'

'Consider it done, sirs. I wanted to let you know I don't have a suit or anything for the funeral. Can I still come?'

'Of course,' I said. 'This will be a funeral like no other.'

'Then I will be happy. Mr Pieter was a good man. A good boss. Always kind to Mother and me. It will be hard to find a replacement for him.'

'I don't think so,' I said. 'Fate has a way of sorting these things out.'

'Thank you, sirs,' he said. 'Sandwiches and beers coming up.'

'I thought we might do a military salute to Pieter,' Stan said. 'Something for Penelope to remember. Assault rifles.'

'We should wear our camouflage outfits,' I said, 'then have a pair of us on each side of the coffin. Blast some shots in the air as the coffin slides into the ocean. It's all starting to come together.'

'Hallelujah,' said Bull with a grin. 'But fingers crossed.'

* * *

It took me longer than I thought to find a boat. I could have left it to the funeral directors, but this was a special request and everything had to follow the plan — there might be some last-minute changes that needed to be taken into account. I could have delegated it to Stan, but he would have ribbed me about the hole I had dug myself into. I'd got enough teasing from Bull; I wasn't adding Stan to the list.

The main problem was the carrying of a corpse on the boat. It was the Zulu equivalent of bad karma. This sort of request had to be sanctified by the local medicine man, and that took money, which was no problem, and time, which was. It would take a week at least, I was told. In the end, I agreed to a deal with a local expat from Germany, whose breath smelled like a whisky barrel and who had no religious reason not to pick up a large tax-free bonus for a couple of hours' sailing.

I spent half an hour speaking to the funeral directors about the change of plans. Their doubts were assuaged by doubling the cost that we had earlier agreed. I felt like a puppet whose strings were being pulled. The irony was that it was me who had come up with the plan that was unravelling before my very eyes.

Stan had organised a table that was now set up for six — the four of us plus Penelope and Joni. On it were the remains of the second bottle of vodka, a bottle of red wine to go with the steaks, and a bottle of chilled white for the fish that the ladies were having. Stan fussed around arranging the napkins and cutlery in parallel lines. I slumped into a chair and poured a large slug of vodka. Exquisite. Just what the doctor ordered, or some other cliché, after a frustrating afternoon. Nothing better than a cliché to save the brain searching for something original when it's vodka time.

'Travel plans?' I said. 'What have you ladies arranged?'

'Jesse and I will come back here to say our goodbyes — Jesse said something about the two of you digging around in the office. We've booked a hotel for that night, and will fly home at midday. Should be an easy schedule.'

'And you, Penelope?'

'I've booked a taxi from the harbour straight to the airport,' she said. 'This time tomorrow, I should be back in rainy London, never to return. Too many memories. It's been good while it lasted, but tinged with regrets.'

'The sad moments will fade with time,' I said. 'I'm sure fond memories of Pieter will mostly replace sadness in years to come. We four will never forget our experiences here. I will especially remember the elephants. How stately they seem. How powerful they are. How much they need our protection.'

'The elephants for me, too,' said Red. 'That sense of oneness I felt with them. I will never forget that. Something that Manitou would have said: we are all one small part of the universe — every living thing tied up together.'

'For me,' said Stan, 'it will be the elation of the battle on the west fence, and the desolation when we arrived back here to find the camp taken by the poachers. Two sides of the same coin that Fate tosses in the air for you. You can never be sure of the outcome.'

'And you, Bull?' Joni asked.

'Easy,' he said. 'It's this boy here. The potential within him. Where Red bonded with the elephants, I did so with Ibo. I'd like to come back in a year's time and see how he has matured. Every one of us has made a difference during our time here. We'll go home with our heads held high. Not many people can say that.'

I placed my right hand on the middle of the table. 'All for one and one for all,' I said.

Three hands were placed on mine.

CHAPTER TWENTY

'Pieter,' I said. 'What can I tell you about Pieter?'

The limousines had picked us all up and we had travelled to the boat in convoy behind the hearse. I was in the lead car with Penelope, Joni and Jesse. My three friends were in the second car and everybody from the safari business in the third. We'd arrived at the harbour carrying the coffin, and now stood to attention each side of it on a plank on the boat. The German's breath had added garlic today to go with the whisky fumes — be good not to linger on. I wondered just how many passengers were willing to put up with the fumes and get on board.

Ibo came up to the four of us and handed us the assault rifles for the ceremonial firing of the salute after my speech was finished. Penelope, standing at the foot of the coffin dabbed at her eyes with a white handkerchief. Her mascara had run, and Joni wiped it off and then held her hand.

'He was tortured by the Russian mafia,' I said. 'Only the four of us know that. He didn't act badly under pressure. We were always proud of him for that. He was a hero over many battles and we each owe him a debt of gratitude for the times he saved our lives.

'A true friend,' I continued. 'Not many people can say that about a person. When he goes to heaven, he will be sorely missed. After giving up being a mercenary, like all of us, he made a new life. He embraced the game reserve and made it his home and surrounded himself with loyal colleagues. What might he miss? Munty's cooking, Ibo's attention and the steadfastness of his rangers. The animals have been protected by his care, and that may be his lasting gift to them.

'Not perfect — that's for sure — but even his sins may have given a moment of happiness to the ladies who benefited from the love he gave to each and every one of them. Penelope is a living witness to that. After only knowing Pieter for just two weeks, she knew that he was the man to marry, to make her life whole. Now that will not happen.'

Penelope gave a deep-throated sob, and Joni wrapped a protective arm around her. Jesse, as sharp as a needle, looked at me, seeking an answer. I gave him the briefest of smiles, which I was sure he would understand.

'And so it is,' I said in conclusion, 'that we send this coffin to the bottom of the ocean.'

The German raised the plank and the coffin slid downwards to its resting place. We four stood to attention and fired the assault rifles into the air. It was over.

I breathed out. It had all come together, after all.

The boat started to chug back to the quay and merely fifteen minutes later we stood on the side where the cars waited. A taxi arrived to take Penelope to the airport, and we transferred her suitcase from the lead car to the cab. I kissed her on the cheek and told her to be strong. The taxi rolled away into the horizon.

I told everyone I would see them back at the camp and that Jesse, Joni and I had a stop to make en route. We climbed in and set off.

The car pulled into the fire station grounds and I got out. Jesse climbed out too. 'I think I'd like to come with you.'

Together we made our way inside. A firefighter smiled at us and told us to go upstairs to the canteen. Inside, a man was sitting at a table drinking coffee. He turned around.

'Has she gone?' said Pieter.

'I knew it,' said Jesse.

'You owe me big time, Pieter,' I said. 'Yes, she's gone back home, flight leaving in an hour so.'

'I can breathe again, then?' Pieter said.

'There's still work to be done,' I said. 'We have to give you a new identity. Change your name on everything relating to the reserve and the safaris, so Penelope doesn't realise what we've done. You have some explaining to do with the staff, too. None of them knew what we were doing. They might have sought a session with the local medicine man, to get some sort of blessing for you.'

'And you and I need to talk,' said Jesse. 'I may have a proposition to put to you.'

'How did you know, Jesse?' I said.

'You're not a man who likes to tell lies,' he said. 'When you first told us about Pieter, and in today's speech, you never actually said he was dead. You skirted around talking about him and death. Even today when the time came, you spoke of sending "the coffin" into the ocean — you didn't say "his body". You've got a sneaky streak to you, but there are good intentions behind it. Let's get back and do some business. And I need a big glass of bourbon.'

We climbed inside the car and set off back to the camp. We couldn't see much through the darkened windows, but what I did see made me realise I liked the country. It had some bad points, but a lot of good, too. People cared about it. It was their country, rich or poor, and they would defend it. It needed more opportunities for the people, for sure, but that would come about as the country itself grew. Time would sort that out. Pieter would have a good life here, doing a job he liked. That had value. He was a lucky man.

There were gasps when we got back and Pieter stepped out of the car. The rangers, a superstitious bunch, stepped back in a mixture of disbelief and horror. I walked over to the drinks table and poured Jesse a bourbon over ice, a white wine for Joni and a beer for myself. We joined the rest of the crew, who were sitting smiling and drinking their beer.

'You're a lucky man, Johnny,' Bull said. 'You could sell sand in the desert. How you managed to pull it off, I don't know. It looked touch and go for a while. You've got an honest face, maybe that's it. Don't get too big-headed about it though. Smug doesn't suit you.'

'Could you see Pieter settling down with Penelope?' I said. 'I'd have given it a week before he was tearing his hair out. A fortnight till he was digging an escape tunnel. I hope he's learned a lesson. But will he change? I doubt it. Pieter will always be Pieter, but I love him for that. "As constant as the northern star", as Shakespeare put it.'

'Julius Caesar,' Bull said. 'Anything you can do I can do better.'

'OK,' I said. 'Who won the FA Cup in 1943?'

'How should I know that?'

'Because it's significant,' I said. 'It was wartime and there was no contest. Just like now, no contest.'

'So sneaky,' he said. 'Should be your calling card. Sneaky Silver. Has a certain ring about it. What do you think, Jesse?'

'Definitely,' he said. 'Got away with murder. A good trait to have. How much longer is Pieter going to be? We have business to do, although I suspect everything will be irrelevant. I want to buy this place, and I know what my financial guys will say. They'll say only a lunatic would do that. Likely to be a money pit. But think what this could be for entertaining our top clients. An experience like no other, and you could set up team-building exercises, too. We could easily factor that in. My gut tells me it's a good investment, and my gut is rarely wrong.'

'And what do you feel, Joni?' Bull said.

'It will be a big change of lifestyle,' she said, 'but it would be fun. Give it a go is what I think. When Jesse has a vision, you have to trust it. There'll be a lot to do, but we could make this place something special. I'm with you, Jesse. As ever.'

She reached out and placed her hand on his. A gesture of unconditional love. Jesse was lucky to have her.

'I'll do it on one condition,' Jesse said. 'And that is that you, Johnny, say the eulogy at my funeral. I have no children to hand the task to, and you and I have bonded in such a short time. It's something special. After what you said today, you'd make a decent job of it. Maybe embroider the truth a little?'

'I can think of worse conditions,' I said. 'I would be truly honoured.'

'I have a wish,' said Bull. 'And here he comes.'

Ibo came up to us and asked whether there was anything he could do, rather than us having to get up. It was a mixed barbecue — impala, kudu, beef kebabs — so a slice of each to start?

'A great idea,' said Bull. 'Maybe raid the wine cupboard and see if there's a special red to go with it.'

'Yes, sirs,' Ibo said.

'Heart over head?' I said.

'Sometimes you score a maximum on both counts,' Bull said.

'You've grown fond of the boy,' said Jesse. 'What is it you want for him? I'm in a good mood, so now's a great time to ask.'

'He's an uncut diamond,' Bull said. 'Can't read or write much, but with a little polishing could be a great asset here. Maybe as a ranger, maybe some role inside the lodge. Being polished means some investment. He needs education and that costs money. I'm ready to chip in. What do you think, Jesse?'

'I'll go with your recommendation,' said Jesse. 'If that's your feeling, I trust you. I'll back him.'

'I know someone who might be of use to you in setting up the new operation,' I said. 'I have a suspicion that Pieter's bookkeeping skills may be a little thin. He's a guy called Nick Shannon. He's a forensic accountant.'

Jesse's expression was blank.

'Basically, he's a fraud detective. He has a young guy that he's training up. The guy's name is Valentine, and he spends a lot of time looking at accounts. I suspect he'd jump at the opportunity to spend a while out here, getting everything into place so that you know whether you're making a profit and how to remedy things if you're not. Shannon would regard it as part of Valentine's training — broaden his horizons. Even if he didn't see it that way, he'd do it as a favour to me. Shannon and I have a brotherly bond — it's a long story.'

'Seems things are falling into place,' said Jesse. 'I'm getting the feeling that this deal is meant to be.'

Pieter got another table and chair and joined us.

'Everyone happy?' I said.

'They all saw why we did it,' he said. 'Penelope didn't make any friends among the staff, it seems.'

'And that surprised you?'

'All water under the bridge now,' he said.

'Just a reminder,' I said. 'You owe us big time.'

'I'm eternally grateful,' he said. 'How do I get myself into these situations?'

'We've been asking that for years,' I said. 'Maybe it's finally sunk in. Right, Pieter, you need to show Jesse the paperwork before the meal arrives.'

'By paperwork,' he said, 'you mean what exactly?'

My heart sank. 'Accounts. Stuff going out and stuff coming in.'

'Van Lloyd used to handle all that.'

'Then I think you need a new skill set,' I said. 'Do the best you can in the next fifteen minutes. We'll have to tap dance after that — make it up as we go along.'

'Situation normal, then,' said Bull.

Jesse and Pieter went off to the office.

I turned to Joni. 'Jesse's a lucky man to have such a supportive wife.'

'I do my best to make him happy,' she said. 'Sometimes it's not easy, but he's a good man and I will miss him when the time comes for him to pass over. Let's give him all the pleasure we can, in the meantime.'

The food arrived and was a carnivore's dream. Ibo refilled our drinks and we settled down for our last night together. Red told us about Manitou and Stan talked about his homeland of Poland. Bull and I ribbed each other on something or other, as ever. A taxi arrived to take Jesse and Joni to their hotel — luxury at last for them. I kissed Joni on her cheek and pulled Jesse into a bear hug.

'I hope it all goes well in the future, old man,' I said. 'Anything you need, just call. We'll all be there for you.'

'Who would have thought it,' he said. 'A simple safari — and boy, was this safari simple — turns into all this. The adventure of a lifetime. The irony of it is that no one will believe me when I tell them about it. You couldn't make it up. Hell, I think I've made some good friends here. You guys look after yourselves.'

'And you, too,' I said.

The taxi tooted its horn and they got in. They waved goodbye as the taxi drove off.

Another chapter of my life done.

CHAPTER TWENTY-ONE

Pieter came with us to the airport and the five of us sat drinking espressos landside in the first-class lounge. We were quiet for a while and there was a sadness between us.

'What we have is too big to let go,' I eventually said. 'We mustn't let it go so long. We only seem to meet in adversity, and that's not good enough. We need to meet up in person each year, or maybe every six months. Just some time to meet up again as friends, rather than having to shoot some people for a reason to get together.'

'Come and stay with me at my hotel by the lake,' Stan said. 'Drink some of the best vodka and eat pickled gherkins. My treat first, and the rest of you can take it from there.'

'Have some Texas sun and ride a few horses,' said Red.

'Then time for us to entertain on St Jude,' Bull said. 'An easy lifestyle when the world becomes too much to bear. Fish for big game.'

'And sit in the sun drinking rum punches,' I said. 'An escape from the worries of everyday life. We're getting older. Sooner or later, our reflexes will get slower. Sooner or later, we'll get more of the shakes when raising a gun against a living foe. We're on the slippery slope.'

'Hell,' said Pieter. 'I think we're good for another few years.'

'I would like to think that,' I said, 'but when the next time comes, we should look at the situation afresh. Is it too much to risk? Is it worth leaving one's family to put us in danger, to settle a score? Maybe just the threat of us will deter those who would fight against us. More than that needs heavy thought. I've got a wife and twins. How much will they be affected if I never come back?'

'I'll echo that,' Bull said. 'I have a good life and would not want to do anything to jeopardise that. I've got enough money left from what we earned in Amsterdam to fall back on. Enough to make me happy in comfort for those retirement years. It's going to take a lot for me to sacrifice that.'

'Ever heard the word "melancholy"?' I said. 'That's where we are at the moment. Time will move on. But I hope none of us feels that this has been a wasted experience. We've saved some animals, and revived a business that had resorted to poaching to stay rich. I feel proud of what we did. I will never look at an elephant again in the same way. A rhino, too. Come to think of it, all the animals. We leave them in your hands, Pieter.'

The information on the screen announced my flight — which was Bull's, too — was due for boarding. We stood up. Pieter, Stan and Red stood, too.

'Get away with you,' I said. 'You know I don't do sentimental.'

'First time I've agreed with Johnny for years,' Bull said. 'Look after yourselves, and if you can't, we're here to help. One last hug, and then, as the big man said, get on with you.'

We did a big group hug.

Bull and I walked through to the small queue for our first-class flight.

'Hope the champagne is good,' said Bull, 'because I need a large glass of something or other.'

'Amen,' I said.

CHAPTER TWENTY-TWO

Bull and I got off the hotel's shuttle boat from Barbados and walked along the sand. Home. Safe. I let it all wrap around me and comfort me.

Anna and Bull's wife, Mai Ling, were at the beach bar waiting for us. Our children were playing in the sand, contented. They looked up when we got close, ran towards us and flung themselves into our arms. Anna stood there watching the scene and burst into tears.

'You're back,' she said.

'Would seem so.'

'Don't get smart with me, Johnny Silver. Mai Ling and I have been worried sick. Half the time we can't talk on the phone because there's no signal. The other half we can't tell if what you say is true, that you're not in danger. This has got to stop, Johnny. No more adventures. Come on, give me a kiss and hold me tight. I missed you so much.'

We stood, closely entwined, on the sand. There's nothing better than true love.

'I promise, Anna,' I said. 'No more being away from you. No more adventures. It stops now. This is the end.'

I uncrossed my fingers.

THE END

THE JOFFE BOOKS STORY

We began in 2014 when Jasper agreed to publish his mum's much-rejected romance novel and it became a bestseller.

Since then we've grown into the largest independent publisher in the UK. We're extremely proud to publish some of the very best writers in the world, including Joy Ellis, Faith Martin, Caro Ramsay, Helen Forrester, Simon Brett and Robert Goddard. Everyone at Joffe Books loves reading and we never forget that it all begins with the magic of an author telling a story.

We are proud to publish talented first-time authors, as well as established writers whose books we love introducing to a new generation of readers.

We won Trade Publisher of the Year at the Independent Publishing Awards in 2023. We have been shortlisted for Independent Publisher of the Year at the British Book Awards for the last four years, and were shortlisted for the Diversity and Inclusivity Award at the 2022 Independent Publishing Awards. In 2023 we were shortlisted for Publisher of the Year at the RNA Industry Awards.

We built this company with your help, and we love to hear from you, so please email us about absolutely anything bookish at feedback@joffebooks.com

If you want to receive free books every Friday and hear about all our new releases, join our mailing list: www.joffebooks.com/contact

And when you tell your friends about us, just remember: it's pronounced Joffe as in coffee or toffee!